"Don't call me lord. Do you understand?"

She glanced up at him in surprise before quickly looking down again. "What shall I call you then, my l. . . ?" She stopped, biting her lip in confusion.

"My name is Decimus," he told her softly.

Frowning, she answered him slowly. "I. . .I cannot call you by your name!"

"It's my name, and it's what I prefer." Decimus began to feel impatient.

"But I am a slave. It's not proper."

"Look." Decimus brushed a hand in agitation through his tousled blond locks. How could he explain to the girl without sounding like some raving lunatic? "You're not a slave. I mean. . .well, you were. . .but you're not. I don't want a slave."

Her head remained bent and her voice seemed small and far away. "You don't want me?"

Rolling his eyes heavenward and releasing a sigh, Decimus was at a loss for words. *God, help me. If You wanted this, I need some guidance.*

DARLENE MINDRUP is a full-time homemaker and home school teacher. A "radical feminist" turned "radical Christian," Darlene lives in Arizona with her husband and two children. She believes "romance is for everyone, not just the young and beautiful."

Books by Darlene Mindrup

HEARTSONG PRESENTS
HP207—The Eagle and the Lamb

Edge
of Destiny

Darlene Mindrup

Heartsong Presents

*To my children, Dena and Devon, who have given
my life focus for the last eighteen years. May
God always hold them in the palm of His hand.*

*And to Anita Johnson, who has taught me the
true meaning of friendship.*

A note from the Author:
*I love to hear from my readers! You may write to me at
the following address:* **Darlene Mindrup
Author Relations
P.O. Box 719
Uhrichsville, OH 44683**

ISBN 1-57748-008-2

EDGE OF DESTINY

All of the characters and events in this book are fictitious.
Any resemblance to actual persons, living or dead, or to
actual events is purely coincidental.

Cover illustration by Brian Bowman.

PRINTED IN THE U.S.A.

one

Decimus Antigonus stood on the edge of the milling crowd and felt his stomach coil with revulsion. As large as the city of Rome was, how had he managed to be at this particular spot during this moment in time? Would that he were anywhere else in this whole stinking city.

"I am bid ten denarii. Do I hear more?" The crusty slave master spread out his toothless smile across the crowd.

"Eleven denarii." The speaker threw an angry glare across the gathering throng, challenging a man on the other side.

The man looked calmly back, his obsidian gaze unblinking. His robes denoted his occupation, a priest in one of the temples.

As the afternoon sun beat down upon his back, Decimus studied the dark-eyed priest. Knowing what the man had in store for his unfortunate victim, Decimus felt a wave of pity. Whether they were male or female, most of the slaves in the temples were destined for prostitution.

"Twelve denarii." The priest's cool voice and dark look sent a shiver down Decimus' back. Evil seemed to emanate from the man in waves.

Murmurs broke out among the crowd. Obviously a war was going on over the girl standing on the auction block. The slave dealer standing beside her smiled his gapped grin and his eyes began to gleam.

Decimus' eyes went to the girl standing resolutely on the platform. Small of stature, thin and emaciated, he could find no reason for the avid bidding.

Then his eyes lifted to the girl's face and held. The only feature that redeemed her face from plainness was the large brown eyes that gazed out at the crowd fearfully. Dark lashes swept down to once again obscure her eyes and the terror that was lurking there.

The bidding had reached twenty denarii. Decimus stared in surprise at the young girl. What did these men see that he could not? True, her coloring was unusual. Blond hair very much the color of his own topped a rather petite frame that looked as though a good gust of wind would blow it away. Blond hair and brown eyes were indeed a striking combination, but for twenty denarii?

For a moment the girl's eyes lifted and stared straight into his own, and then Decimus knew. Purity and innocence reached out to him, touching his very soul. Surely the angels in heaven must have such eyes. How had such a girl managed to make it to the slave market of Rome and still retain such innocence?

The girl's vulnerability touched Decimus on the raw. Flicking a glance across the crowd, he could see the merchant's face as the priest continued to outbid him. The man wanted the girl badly, that much was obvious. The hotness of his gaze as it roved the girl's body caused a slow boil of anger to erupt inside of Decimus.

Looking across at the priest, Decimus could see no change in his demeanor. The priest was as cool and confident as ever. When the priest looked at the girl, it was for an entirely different reason. As a temple prostitute, the girl would bring a fortune, at least until her purity was stripped away by the atrocities committed there. The desire to possess such innocence would be overwhelming to many of the men of Rome who were sated with the sins of this life.

The crowd had become almost hushed as the contest continued. A third man had entered the bidding. Decimus recognized one of the more prominent senators of Rome, the purple trim of his tunic giving evidence of his aristocracy. One look into the girl's eyes and the senator had entered the fray.

Decimus glanced back at the girl. Her body was visibly shaking. *If only she would keep her eyes down,* he thought to himself, for there was little else to recommend her.

Where had he seen eyes like that before? A sudden image came to his mind of a young Jewish girl with brown hair and dark brown eyes much the same as those he had just seen. *Sara.*

Decimus felt a tightening in his chest. Sara. A slave girl in his previous master's house. A slight smile touched his lips. Sara had no looks to speak of either. Her beauty had come from within, but that inner loveliness had been so great that Decimus the slave had fallen in love. That sort of beauty of spirit could only come from the Spirit of God. Seeing the girl on the auction block, Decimus realized that she and Sara had much in common.

The ache in Decimus' chest grew even tighter. He still loved Sara. He had asked her to marry him, but she had refused. She had told him that his love was a brother's for a sister. Not so, for hadn't he stayed faithful to her memory all these years? But was her memory as clear in his mind as it once was? He was no longer sure. He had not seen Sara for almost five years, and his feelings were confused.

"Thirty denarii," the slave merchant cackled gleefully, bringing Decimus abruptly back to the present. "Do I hear more?" Rubbing his hands together, he glanced from the portly merchant to the priest. *The senator must have the upper hand,* Decimus decided.

Obviously both the merchant and the priest were reaching the end of their resources. Sweat was beaded across the merchant's brow as he wrung his hands in agitation. Only the priest remained unaffected. The senator was smiling smugly. Only a miracle would save the girl now.

Decimus heart ached for the girl. Whichever way she went she would be misused and abused, her innocence defiled. *God, help her,* he pled.

His thoughts were interrupted by a woman making her way through the crowd. Her bright yellow palla would have drawn attention even if her regal bearing had not. She wasn't old, but neither was she young. In her youth she had probably rivaled

Aphrodite in beauty. She went to the senator and touched his arm, turning to see where his attention was focused.

When the senator looked down at her, his face was immediately filled with shame. Decimus could see even at this distance the love that glowed from his eyes as he beheld what must have been his wife. She frowned reproachfully at him before she turned and walked away. The senator flicked a brief look at the slave girl before turning and hurrying after her.

So much for the senator. Decimus would much rather have seen the girl go to him than to either of the others, but God had apparently saved at least one Roman from the sin of adultery.

Now the priest's eyes were gleaming with an unholy light. Decimus knew that although the priest would probably have more money than the merchant, too much spent on one slave could cause him to be punished. He couldn't have defeated the senator, but the merchant was another matter.

The girl was devoid of color, her lips trembling noticeably. A tear was coursing a path through the dust on her cheeks. In her innocence, was she aware of what was intended for her? The anger within Decimus began to churn. Grinding his teeth together, his gaze again went from merchant to priest.

The crowd had grown larger and although no one else had entered the bidding, many were taking sides. The chattering around him grew unbearably loud and the press of unwashed humanity against him from all sides made Decimus want to wretch. He should leave. He had a very important appointment with a man who could help him leave this accursed city. Still, something held him in place.

The merchant glared angrily at the priest, his color an alarming puce. The priest gazed back at him impassively.

So, the priest had won. Decimus felt his skin begin to crawl as he recognized the symbol of the gold necklace glinting in the sunlight. A snake curved round a pole. The symbol of Aesculapius, the god of healing. People went to the temple of Asklepion and allowed snakes to crawl all over their bodies, hoping for healing. Decimus closed his eyes tightly. Were all

Romans insane? If only they could know the *true* Healer, the One who heals the spirit. Many of the diseases of these people came from their own immoral lifestyles.

"Going once."

The slave merchant's voice brought Decimus back to reality. So what price had the priest paid? He had missed the last bid.

"Going twice." The slave trader glanced hopefully at the merchant and then over the crowd. Although the girl had already brought what amounted to a fortune in terms of slave prices, he still hoped for more. "Surely you can see the worth of such a piece. She has much to offer."

When Decimus glanced at the girl, he found her staring back at him. Her luminous brown eyes seemed to reach into his very soul and found him lacking. Sadly, she lowered her eyes, submissively accepting her fate.

Without realizing it, Decimus found himself moving forward to the fringe of the crowd. The slave master was raising his hand for the final call. The merchant had turned away, pushing through the crowd, his face as scarlet as the tunic he wore. The priest stared impassively at the girl, his eyes glowing black.

Decimus felt helpless as he watched the slave trader's hand raised to its utmost. Cold sweat broke out across his forehead. *Forget it,* he told himself angrily. *She's nothing to you.* Why should he feel such agony over an unknown slave girl?

"One hundred denarii." The crowd around Decimus parted, surprised faces turned his way. A rippling murmur ran through the mob.

For the first time since the whole procedure began, Decimus saw the priest's face become animated. His mouth dropped open, his jaws working convulsively. His eyebrows flew toward his receding hairline and his eyes lost their impassivity. He glared in angry surprise at Decimus, who was no less surprised himself.

After one startled glance at Decimus, the slave trader asked again for a higher bid. The heat from the sun seemed to intensify as Decimus felt the sweat break out on his palms. After what seemed an eternity, the priest swung angrily away and the slave trader turned back to Decimus.

"My lord, she is yours," he announced hesitantly, his look passing over Decimus' worn clothes. Since leaving Ephesus, Decimus had dressed in rags, hoping to convince any would-be robbers that he was too poor to be bothered. Now, everyone in the crowd would know that was not so, and Decimus knew that among such a crowd there would be cunning thieves and robbers.

Lifting his chin, Decimus strode forward, stopping in front of the podium. He jerked his money bag from inside his tunic where it had rested peaceably for years. He still had much of the money Antonius had given him when he had sent him away with his freedom. If he kept this up, though, his fortune would dwindle away like the sands of time.

Decimus handed over the coins to the slave trader, making sure he received his bill of sale and slave papers. Now he was really aggravated with himself. What was he going to do with a slave? Especially a scrawny little girl.

For the first time since he had opened his mouth and uttered those preposterous words, he looked at the girl. Although her lashes veiled her eyes, a slight smile curved her lips and her trembling had ceased.

What was she thinking? That she was safe with him? How could she be so accepting of her fate?

His mind wandered back to when the Romans had invaded his homeland of Britannia. He did not know if his family were even still alive. The last he had seen of his family was his father lying in a pool of blood, his mother's prostrate form over his father, and his sister being shoved from one Roman soldier to another while they laughed at her torment.

He had tried to come to her defense, but a young lad of ten had very little strength compared to a seasoned Roman soldier.

Decimus had managed to draw blood from one hearty specimen with his teeth before he was knocked senseless.

Many beatings later, he had finally been cowed. Most of the scars were still visible across his back. Even now he squirmed when he thought of his cowardice. He had been born a warrior, one of Britannia's aristocracy. Wouldn't it have been better to die a free man than live as a slave?

But stay. If he had died then, he would never have heard the Good News of Christ. No, even now he would rather be a slave that knew Christ rather than a free person who was a slave to sin.

But this girl. What had she undergone to stand there so meekly willing to succumb to her fate, and what was he to do with her now? He should have minded his own business and bypassed the crowd, but curiosity had gotten the best of him.

Now here he was expected at a meeting, a rather dangerous liaison at that—and he was encumbered with a female slave! *God, what am I to do now?*

Decimus helped the girl down from the platform, avoiding her eyes. Long, blond hair draped demurely across her cheeks. Why was her head not shaved? Obviously, she hadn't been sent to the baths as slaves usually were before they were brought to market.

He tapped his foot impatiently while the slaver removed the iron leg bands. Taking the girl by the arm, Decimus propelled her none too gently through the crowd. His one aim was to get as far away from the central market as quickly as possible. The snickers that followed him sent waves of color washing across his face.

When they were clear of the marketplace, Decimus pulled the girl to a stop in the shade of an apartment building. He glanced quickly around to see if they had been followed. Seeing no one, he turned his attention back to the girl.

Her face was bent submissively down, while her fingers toyed with the frayed cord around her waist. The rough brown wool of her dress could barely be called a tunic. As his eyes moved over her he noticed other things he hadn't noticed before. She was barefoot and bleeding. Decimus bent to inspect the sores on her feet.

"You're hurt."

"It's no matter, my lord." Her voice flowed over him in gentle waves.

Decimus allowed himself to look into her eyes. As he expected, their light spoke volumes. Shaking his head, he quickly got to his feet.

"We can't stop here. Someone may be watching." He looked at her skeptically. He hated to cause her more pain, but they couldn't stay here. "Do you think you can keep up with me? We're going to have to move fast."

"I am strong, my lord," she answered softly. "I will keep up."

Grunting, Decimus started to turn away before he remembered something. "I don't know your name."

"Chara, my lord. My name is Chara."

Decimus said nothing for a moment. Finally he nodded his head. "Chara," he said, seeming to test the word on his tongue. "That's a beautiful name." She didn't answer and he frowned. "One other thing. Don't call me lord. Do you understand?"

She glanced up at him in surprise before quickly looking down again. "What shall I call you then, my l. . .?" She stopped, biting her lip in confusion.

"My name is Decimus," he told her softly.

Frowning, she answered him slowly. "I. . .I cannot call you by your name!"

"It's my name, and it's what I prefer." Decimus began to feel impatient.

"But I am a slave. It's not proper."

"Look." Decimus brushed a hand in agitation through his tousled blond locks. How could he explain to the girl without sounding like some raving lunatic? "You're not a slave. I mean . . .well, you were. . .but you're not. I don't want a slave."

Her head remained bent and her voice seemed small and far away. "You don't want me?"

Rolling his eyes heavenward and releasing a sigh, Decimus was at a loss for words. *God, help me. If You wanted this, I need some guidance.*

He looked uneasily around him. "We'll have to talk about this later. Right now we have to get out of here. Are you sure you can walk?"

"Yes."

Taking her again by the arm, Decimus began to hurry her toward the other end of the city. The sundial at the town square had shown him that the hour was later than he expected. The sun would be going down quickly and he still had a long way to go.

When they reached a high white wall, Decimus slowed his steps. Glancing around him again, he opened the gate in the wall and ushered Chara ahead of him. Flowering hibiscus lent their color to the already fading blooms of other flowers. Summer was full upon them, as was evidenced by the dry petals of the wilting leaves. A marble fountain splashed in the center of the enclosed garden, shaded by a large olive tree.

Decimus led Chara to a marble bench beside the fountain. "Wait here," he told her.

He was gone only a moment, returning with an elderly gentleman dressed in the tunic of the Roman aristocracy. Gentleness emanated from the older man's serene face and a smile lit his features.

"Ah, Decimus. So this is the girl."

Decimus nodded. "I have no idea what to do with her, Antipus. My foolish impulsiveness has imperiled our plans."

Antipus shook his head. "Not at all, my friend. It would take only a moment to rectify the situation."

"I don't understand."

Antipus motioned towards the villa. "Come inside and let's discuss it. It's much too hot out here."

Decimus looked down at Chara. She was still sitting with head bowed, hands clutched together in front of her. Laying a hand on her shoulder, he realized that he was hesitant to leave her.

"Chara is hurt," he told the old man. "She needs tending."

Instantly concerned, Antipus moved to Chara's side. His eyes missed nothing in their quick perusal.

"Of course. I didn't realize." He motioned again towards the villa. "Bring her into the atrium. It's cooler there." Noticing her dirty, disheveled appearance and bloody feet, he paused. "Wait. Better yet, bring her to the baths. I will have one of my servants tend to her while you and I talk."

For some reason he couldn't fathom, Decimus was reluctant to give over care of the girl to someone else. He felt responsible, for one thing, but her obvious fright was another. She had quickly lifted her eyes to his and then dropped them just as quickly, but he had read the fear there. She seemed to trust him even though he had given her no cause, and such faith humbled him.

Reaching down, he scooped the girl into his arms. "Tell me where to go."

Antipus had already started for the house. "Follow me."

He led them through the peristyle and into the atrium. Lush potted plants filled the atrium's room, making it seem as though the garden outside spilled over to the inside. Following Antipus through the hallways, Decimus was struck by the opulent surroundings. Antipus must be one of the higher officials of Rome, and a very wealthy man. He frowned, but kept his thoughts to himself.

The baths were just as luxurious, and profuse potted plants again gave an impression of the airy outside. Pungent scents of sandalwood, myrrh, and a host of other odors he couldn't name, filled the steamy air.

Gently he set Chara on her feet, keeping an arm around her for support. When he glanced down at her, he found her eyes studying his face, but she quickly dropped her gaze.

Antipus clapped his hands and a young girl entered the room. She glanced from Decimus and Chara back to Antipus.

"Take the girl and see to her needs," Antipus told her. "She has need of a clean tunic and see that she gets anything else she may want."

Nodding, the girl came quickly to Chara's side. "This way, my lady."

Chara's head flew up in surprise. "Oh, but I'm not. . ."

"It's all right," Decimus interrupted her. He had no idea what was going to happen or what role the girl might play over the next few days, but he wasn't taking any chances. The less said, the better. "Just do as she says."

When Chara quickly dropped her eyes to the floor, Decimus grew exasperated. Perhaps it was the proper posture for a slave, but it was beginning to get on his already taut nerves. He would have to speak to her about it, but for now it would have to wait.

He followed Antipus from the room and back along the corridors to the atrium. It was definitely cooler in here. Although the open roof allowed the sunshine into the room, the shade from surrounding trees cooled the air as it blew gently through the open portals.

Antipus indicated that Decimus have a seat, and Antipus sat down across from him. He reached for a silver gong sitting on the table, giving it a gentle clang. In answer to his summons, a young man entered the room with a tray of refreshments.

"Please, help yourself," Antipus told Decimus.

Decimus was surprised when his stomach rumbled. "Thank you." He reached for a peach and a knife.

Antipus settled back against the cushions of his seat. "Now, tell me exactly what happened, and how you came to possess a slave."

Getting his thoughts together, Decimus regaled Antipus with his tale from the moment he had entered the market until the time he had fled. Antipus's lips twitched with amusement.

"It's not funny, Antipus," Decimus protested. "What am I going to do with the girl?"

"Settle down, my friend. As I said before, it would take but a moment to set her free. She can remain here if you like."

For some reason Decimus was reluctant to commit himself to such an action. He knew it was the right thing to do; then why did he hesitate? Instead, he changed the subject. "What was your idea for getting me out of Rome?"

The old man pursed his lips, taking his time before answering. Lifting a pear from the plate, he began to methodically cut it into sections.

Decimus could barely contain his impatience. He felt like ripping the fruit from the man's hands and demanding an explanation. He managed to control himself, but only just.

Antipus leaned forward, his expression serious. "One of the main problems we have with leaving the country at this time is that the Romans have learned that Christians won't lie, or deny their Lord."

"And?"

"Patience, my friend. If you would let me explain without interrupting?"

Leaning back, Decimus forced himself to relax. "I'm sorry. Please continue."

"The Romans also know that a Christian won't own a slave."

When Decimus opened his mouth, Antipus fixed him with a look, and Decimus subsided.

"The soldiers have become devious in their ways of sniffing out Christians. Anyone who boards a ship is asked if he is one." He leaned forward to emphasize his point. "But, if you board a ship and they know you *are* a slave they will likely not bother you."

Decimus rose slowly to his feet. "Are you suggesting that I become a slave to escape Rome? Because if you are, you must be out of your mind! I will never again bow to the yoke of any man, nor will I ever subject anyone else to it." He shook his head angrily. "No, Antipus, I will never be any man's slave again, nor do I ever intend to own one."

Antipus raised his brows. "But you already do."

Sinking back to the couch, Decimus put his head in his hands. He had already forgotten this afternoon's fiasco. "What a mess I've made of things."

"Decimus, listen to me. I know how you feel, and I admire you for it. No one could fault you for your compassion where the girl is concerned. Probably I would have done the same in your situation." He grinned. "I have done so on occasion myself, purchasing slaves here or there and then giving them their freedom." He watched Decimus carefully. "None of the servants in my house are slaves. They have all been granted their freedom and may leave anytime they choose."

Surprised, Decimus searched the old man's face for the truth of the statement.

"Chara will be safe with me." Antipus suddenly sobered. "I wish I could say the same for my own wife. The more I become involved with clandestine Christian affairs, the greater the risk of detection. I would ask that you take my wife with you, but that would certainly bring notice to me, and it's not yet time. I need to help as many others as I can to escape from this city. I'm not sure how, but I'll find a way." He stared thoughtfully at his twisted fingers. "My only fear is for the safety of Agrippina. As my wife, she will be subject to the same punishment I receive."

"What of Chara, then? What would happen to her were you to be arrested?" Decimus queried in concern.

Antipus glanced up. "What? Oh, yes. She would be sold on the slave market again as would any others in this household." He smiled without mirth. "Of course, my servants know that if anything happens, they are to run as far and as fast as they possibly can. I wouldn't wish any of them to become lion feed, nor a human torch in Nero's gardens, for that matter."

"Nero is an animal," Decimus declared vehemently.

"No," Antipus answered gently. "Nero is a devil. If I believed it possible, I would say he was Satan incarnate." Shaking his head sadly, his eyes took on a preoccupied look. "What has happened to the glory of Rome? What went wrong? That the people can worship a man as a god. And such a man! Someone who would kill his own mother and wife and then marry a prostitute. Is anywhere safe from such a madman?"

"Rome has tentacles everywhere, but less so in Britannia," Decimus declared. "I don't remember much about my birth country, but I know that it is far enough away that Rome has less concern with it."

"I wouldn't be too sure," Antipus answered. "Since Nero forced Seneca to commit suicide, more and more his generals have the ear of the emperor. They have been stirring up trouble, for they are hungry for conquest."

The young serving boy entered the room. "There is someone to see you at the door, my lord."

Antipus got quickly to his feet. "Ah, the person I've been waiting for. Bring him in."

Decimus came to his feet, the blood draining from his face as the young boy reentered the room, followed by a Roman soldier, impressively dressed in all his regalia.

two

Chara felt the warm, scented waters of the bath drift sooth-
ingly around her as she stepped down the stairs into the tiled
bath. The young girl who had helped her with her things was
lifting a cruse of oil for inspection.

"Would you like a violet scent when you are finished, my
lady?"

Instead of answering her, Chara asked a question of her
own. "What is your name?"

The girl smiled shyly. "Candace, my lady." Again she held
up the cruse, raising her eyebrows questioningly.

What would Decimus have her do? Intuitively Chara knew
something important was going on in the other room. Decimus
had spoken of plans, and both men seemed worried that there
might be danger. He had deliberately stopped her from reveal-
ing to Candace that she was, herself, a slave.

Still, it had been a long time since Chara had been showered
with such attention. And how long had it been since she had a
real bath? She felt the luxurious sensation of the water swirling
around her and reveled in the feel of it. There was no telling
how long it would be before she had such a chance again.

"The violet scent would be nice, Candace, but do you
think you could leave me alone for a while?"

Candace didn't seem surprised. "Of course." She motioned
to a small gong beside the pool. "Just ring that when you're
finished and I will come."

Left on her own, Chara allowed to surface the thoughts she
had been holding at bay. Closing her eyes tightly, she prayed
for continued strength. God had been merciful to her thus
far, but what did her future hold? Why was she being tried in
such a way?

Tears trickled down her cheeks as she thought of her loving mother who had so recently died. Pain washed through her as she once again relived the last eight months.

Her mother had been sick for so long, and her stepfather had taken to drinking and carousing. He had once been an educated and cultured man, but now he would come home at all hours in a drunken stupor, and always her mother forgave him and tried to care for him. But she had been too sick herself.

And Franco, her stepbrother, had only made matters worse. Ever since Chara and her mother had entered the household, Franco had hated her. Perhaps he considered her a usurper who would one day cause him to lose some of his inheritance. Whatever the reason, he had made Chara's life pure misery. But she had refused to tell her mother, knowing that it would only cause dissension and hard feelings.

Then her stepfather had died. In a drunken daze he had managed to fall from the dock into the river. No one had known. Some fishermen had found him one morning washed up on the bank.

After that her mother's health declined even more. Chara attributed that to the fact that upon his father's death, Franco had made it quite clear that Chara and her mother were there only on his forbearance. Chara squirmed at the memory.

And then one morning Chara had gone into her mother's room with her breakfast tray only to find that her mother had died peacefully in the night. Chara grieved, but she had little time to mourn, for Franco had let her know that he wanted nothing to do with Chara, and he began to make her life as hard as possible.

"You're so ugly no decent man would want you," he told her. "And I'm certainly not going to be responsible for you the rest of your life." After that, she had been relegated to the role of servant.

One night Franco had been unusually friendly and invited Chara to dine with him. Although Chara was suspicious, she didn't want to offend him, so she reluctantly accepted. Her stepbrother had been charming, lulling Chara into a false sense of security. Perhaps he had had a change of heart. It was only later that she found out that he had slipped a potion into her drink that would make her sleep.

When she awakened, she found herself in leg chains far from her home of Gaul. Franco had sold her to a slave trader heading for Rome. The journey had been long and arduous, the heat unbearable. The only thing that had saved her from rape was her constant illnesses.

Chara realized early that something about her seemed to appeal to a particular breed of men, the kind she had no desire to attract. She knew it was not her looks, for she had none to speak of, but something about her drew them nevertheless. She hadn't had to worry about Tarus, the slave trader, for his interest lay elsewhere. He preferred the young boys, and Chara felt sympathy every time Tarus stopped to buy new slaves and a young boy was among them.

Then they had reached Rome, and Tarus decided that rather than spend extra coins on sending the slaves to the baths, he would just stop in the marketplace and hold his own auction.

Chara had learned well the ways of a slave; Tarus had seen to that. When the auction had begun, she had kept her eyes demurely on the ground. She had glanced up once to encounter the gaze of a ruddy-faced merchant, his bright red tunic matching almost to perfection his complexion. She shivered with distaste when he looked into her eyes. His own had grown large, a strange gleam coming into them.

When she heard a second voice entering a bid, she had let curiosity get the best of her and she had looked at the man. His black gaze had rested on her only a moment, but she had felt defiled. His robes had told her that he was a priest, and she shivered at what he probably had in mind for her. Her mother had told her appalling stories of the Romans and their temple prostitutes.

And then she had seen Decimus. His angry blue gaze had

stared into hers, and she felt her heart lurch within her. He was handsome, strongly built. His blond hair shone in the sunlight. Without knowing why, she had longed for him to be the one to purchase her. Realizing from his ragged appearance this could not be so, she still gave way to her imagination. Something about him drew a response from Chara, and she realized that she was making a peremptory judgement. He could be a madman for all she knew, yet there was an indefinable quality about him that spoke of character well hidden.

When a third man had started to bid on her, she had felt mortified with shame. Each man had telling eyes, and what they said caused her to become almost faint with trepidation. She had prayed harder.

In the end, it had been Decimus who had purchased her after all. One hundred denarii! How could he afford so much? His clothes had led her to believe he was just an impoverished bystander. She had hoped for him to purchase her, but now what? What did he have in mind for her?

Pain washed through her when she remembered him saying that he didn't want her. Wasn't that what Franco had told her? But if Decimus didn't want her, why had he paid such an exorbitant price? It didn't make sense, but Chara knew one thing for certain. God had cared for her from the beginning and He surely wouldn't desert her now.

Lifting the silver wand, Chara rang the gong.

❧

Antipus saw the expression on Decimus' face and hastily tried to reassure him. "It's all right, Decimus. Galla is a friend."

Decimus glanced suspiciously from one to the other. Galla stepped forward, extending his arm. Looking from Galla's face to the extended arm, Decimus slowly reached out his own. Galla clasped Decimus' forearm with his hand, and Decimus hesitantly returned the pressure.

Looking relieved, Antipus motioned for them to be seated. "Galla and I have a plan for getting you out of the city."

Decimus' eyes narrowed. "Why would a Roman soldier

want to help me escape from the city?"

Galla regarded him steadily. "Because I am a Christian, too."

"A Roman soldier who is a Christian?" Decimus studied the man warily. "I hope you'll excuse me if I'm not quite convinced."

Smiling, Galla turned to Antipus. "I think our young friend needs some persuading." He turned back to Decimus. "Just what would it take to reassure you?"

Confused, Decimus looked from one man to the other. He shrugged his shoulders helplessly.

Antipus intervened. "Really, Decimus, we only want to help you. Would Marcus have sent you here otherwise?"

Shaking his head, Decimus eyed the other two suspiciously. "I'm sorry, it's just that. . ."

"You are right to trust no one," Galla told him. "Christians are dying every day in the arena because of their faith in their neighbors, and even their own families."

"Please, gentlemen, we haven't much time," Antipus interrupted. "Let's have a seat and discuss all the particulars."

Decimus sat, but his body remained tense. The only reassurance he had that these men were genuine was the word of a close friend. If he couldn't trust these men, he knew of nowhere else to go.

"Decimus has a problem," Antipus told Galla. "He found himself the possessor of a slave today."

Galla's eyebrows rose. "A slave?"

Color flew to Decimus' cheeks, and he hurried to explain the situation. Galla sat back thoughtfully. He looked at Antipus. "Could he not leave the girl with you?"

"I have already suggested that." Antipus told him. "Anyway, I have a plan that might get Decimus out of the city, and perhaps a few others as well."

Galla listened to the old man's suggestion. Pinching his lips between his thumb and finger, he considered a moment. "Your idea has some merit. No one would question a centurion about his slaves." Galla contemplated Decimus, his eyes sparkling with mirth. "And how would you feel being the slave of a Roman centurion?"

Decimus' eyes flickered briefly, but he refused to be baited. "How would I get to Britannia? I have no idea how to get there from here."

Surprised, Galla looked from Antipus to Decimus. "Didn't Antipus tell you? I'll be taking you."

Equally surprised, Decimus glared back at him. "You? Why ever would you be taking me to Britannia?"

"I see Antipus hasn't told you very much."

Antipus smiled slightly, shrugging his shoulders. "I thought I would leave that to you."

Nodding, Galla turned back to Decimus. "Britannia is my home."

Though he was taken aback, Decimus remained silent.

"At least it was the home of my father, and my grandfather and great-grandfather before that. It would take too much time to explain the whole situation," Galla told him. "Let me summarize for you. Many years ago Julius Caesar penetrated my great-grandfather's homeland. My grandfather's father was impressed with the man, but he was also afraid. He sensed that the man had a destiny which would bring him into contact again with Britannia. Later, my grandfather and my father met Claudius, who decided that Britannia would be an asset to Rome. Claudius annexed it into the empire, and for the most part treated my people well. My father decided to accept Claudius's offer of serving in the Roman army."

"He was actually willing to fight against his own people?" Decimus interrupted incredulously.

"At that time peace had been made with Britannia. Claudius made treaties with some of the tribes, and my father was a wise man. He understood the way the winds were blowing, and he knew there would be no stopping the Roman war machine. By serving Rome, my father was planning for the future. But he never forgot Britannia, and he never let me forget it either."

Decimus nodded in understanding. "So, when your father retired, he was granted automatic citizenship, and then when you were born, you were considered a Roman citizen by birth."

Galla nodded. "Correct. And since I have the *privilege* of being a Roman citizen, I have learned much about Rome."

"You're spying for Britannia?"

Sighing, Galla pressed his lips together. "No, I'm not. My father served Rome faithfully, as have I. But since Claudius's murder by his own wife, Rome has become barbarous, wanton in its destruction. Rome is no longer the democracy it was intended to be. It has become vile and depraved. It's time for me to go home. Rome is on its last legs, and the people of Britannia have a chance of regaining what was once lost. I want to help. I also wish to tell them about my Lord, Jesus Christ," he finished quietly. "I have some leave time coming to me, and I wish to visit the home of my father and grandfather."

Decimus couldn't fault the man's logic. He watched him closely, and he liked what he saw. His allegiance was to God, not to Rome. Not even to Britannia. There was strength of purpose in Galla's face. Here was a man of integrity.

"So, what do you say, my friend?" Antipus inquired. "Are you ready to leave Rome? Are you ready, like Galla, to go west and north—and spread God's Word?"

Decimus took his time answering. His look passed from one man to the other. Finally, he nodded his head. "I'm ready!"

"Praise God!"

Three pairs of startled male eyes turned toward the doorway. Chara stood silhouetted within its frame, her hands clutched together in front of her. Her changed appearance was remarkable. A clean white tunic softened her emaciated frame, and her golden hair shone brightly with the reflected light of the now lit torches.

Galla's eyebrows winged upward as his eyes traveled over the young girl standing before him. He turned to Antipus for some answers, but Decimus was already moving forward. He stopped in front of Chara, his eyes full of questions.

Chara's luminous brown eyes returned his look, her face animated with joy. "You know my Lord Jesus!"

Decimus frowned. "What?"

"I heard you just now." She smiled radiantly at Galla. "You know Him, too."

Decimus glanced at Antipus, then at Galla, his look returning to Chara. "You're a Christian?"

Her smile transformed her plain features. "Yes! Oh, praise God that you are one, too. I knew when I saw you in the crowd that there was something different about you." Realizing what she had just said, color flooded Chara's cheeks. Quickly she dropped her eyes to the floor.

Galla looked at Decimus, his lips quirking with humor.

"She's the girl I was telling you about," Decimus told him, his own face coloring with embarrassment.

"The slave?"

Grinding his teeth together in exasperation, Decimus glared at each man in turn. "She's not a slave!" Noting their dubious expressions, he amended his statement. "Well, at least not for long."

Galla was studying Chara, a strange expression on his face. Decimus felt heat run through his body, while at the same time he felt an icy thrill in his midsection. Was this Roman truly a friend? Could he really be trusted? A moment ago he had thought so, but now he wasn't so sure.

Antipus felt the tension emanating from the young Briton and immediately tried to soothe the troubled waters. "Come in, child. Have a seat."

Chara looked to Decimus for permission. Nodding his head, he watched as Chara crossed the room with a rather stiff gait. Remembering the sores on her feet, Decimus followed her and knelt before her. Gently he lifted one foot and then the other, placing them carefully back on the floor.

"The sores don't seem as bad since they've been washed."

Chara murmured her agreement, trying to restore her breathing to normal. The touch of Decimus' hands, so gentle yet so firm, had sent pleasurable tingles running up her legs.

Galla crossed to the couch, taking a seat beside Chara. His encompassing look wandered from head to toe. "So, little sister. How do you come to be in such a position?"

"It's a long story, my lord."

Taking one of her hands, Galla smiled charmingly at her, his soft brown eyes inviting her confidence. "If you are indeed a sister, then surely you know that no man has the right to be called lord, save One."

She smiled into his eyes, feeling for the first time in a long while the freedom to do so. "I'm afraid I have been conditioned to speak so."

"And rather well, I might add," Decimus grunted, somewhat bothered by the exchange. His look wandered over the soldier, and Decimus realized that Galla was not much older than himself. Until now, the thought hadn't occurred to him that the Roman was a mighty handsome specimen, even with that scar running down his cheek. His bronze skin spoke of his health, and his dark, curling hair added to his lean good looks.

Chara told them her story, leaving nothing out. Decimus felt rage begin to bubble inside him. How could any man do that to his own sister, even if she was only a stepsister? If Decimus could have reached the man at that point, he would have gladly flogged him within an inch of his life. He was struggling with shame at such unchristian thoughts when Chara spoke again.

"I hold him no ill will. I can see God's hand in all of this. I was too afraid to leave, even though I knew I wasn't wanted. With Franco, my fear made me more a slave than when I was with Tarus. This way I was forced to leave." She smiled at Decimus. "Now I understand why God has led me here."

Decimus turned away, unwilling that any should see his embarrassment. He was bothered that the girl seemed to have fixated upon him as her personal deliverer.

"Still," Galla spoke gruffly, his hands clenched into fists on his lap, "I would be hard pressed not to hold a grudge."

Antipus thought it time to intervene. Already darkness had descended and they still had resolved nothing. He addressed Chara. "My dear, we have a plan for getting Decimus out of the city and Galla as well. I can see now that I must include you, too."

Suddenly fearful, Chara stared wide-eyed from one to the other. She had the strangest desire to take Decimus' hand and cling to it. Flustered at her unusual reaction, she dropped her lashes over her telling eyes.

"Do you know what is happening to Christians here in Rome?" Antipus asked her gently.

She shook her head solemnly. "I'm afraid that until a few months ago I was rather isolated and protected."

The old man sighed. "Well, I won't regale you with all the gruesome details. Let's just say that Rome has become a very unhealthy place for Christians. Especially since almost a third of the city burned, and many people place the blame on the Christians."

For the next several hours they discussed the details of getting the three out of Rome. Galla would have had no problem on his own, but the others would surely be suspect. As slaves, however, perhaps they would not be bothered.

When they finally agreed on a plan, Antipus rose from his seat. "It's almost midnight. I have had my servants prepare rooms for all of you for the night. You are welcome to stay as long as you wish. Please make yourselves at home. If you need anything, just call one of the servants."

Galla rose with him. "I thank you for the hospitality, but I'm afraid I must decline. I am expected at the garrison." He turned to Decimus. "I'll leave you to make arrangements about clothing for the girl and yourself. Remember, by the time we reach Britannia, cold weather will be setting in."

Decimus nodded. "I'll see to it."

Antipus followed Galla out the door, leaving Decimus and

Chara alone. Decimus picked up a marble statue of a horse and began to twirl it nervously in his fingers. Finally, he cleared his throat.

"We have assumed that you wish to go with us to Britannia, but if this is not so, you have only to say."

"You forget that despite what you say, I am still a slave," she answered quietly.

Thunking the statue back on the table, Decimus frowned. "Just for the moment." He stopped, remembering the plans they had just discussed. He was bothered more than a little bit by the fact that Chara would be considered the property of the Roman. That troubled him more than the fact that *he* would be considered so, also.

Chara looked down at the floor, allowing her hair to fall forward over her cheeks. She said nothing for a long time and Decimus took the time to study her. Although her face was hidden from view, the rest of her was clearly visible. She didn't look more than sixteen, though her incarceration could have added years to her appearance. How old *was* the child?

Her hair shone golden after her bath, even lighter than he had at first believed. She had the coloring of someone from Germania and he wondered about her ancestry. The white tunic which hung on her slender figure only added to her air of untouched purity. Bones protruded from her shoulders. Again Decimus felt rage boil inside. Such a gentle girl, yet she had endured so much. Compassion stirred within him, and something else as yet undefinable.

Antipus returned, followed by two servants. "Dagon will show you to your room, Decimus, and Candace will show you yours." He smiled at Chara. "You have had a rough day. I hope you sleep well."

She returned his smile. "Thank you. Thank you for everything."

"I also wish to thank you," Decimus told Antipus before following Dagon out the door.

When they reached the top of the marble staircase, Decimus

stopped, turning Chara toward him. "You will be all right?"

For a moment she stared deeply into his eyes. Placing her hands gently on his shoulders, she raised on her tiptoes and softly kissed him on the lips. "Thank God He sent you into my life."

Decimus was moved despite himself. He didn't want to be responsible for this girl, and yet here he was making plans for her to go with him to Britannia. He didn't want to feel anything for her, and yet he had been stirred by her guileless kiss. Letting go of her shoulders, he turned and quickly exited, following Dagon down the corridor.

Chara watched him walk away, a sinking sensation in the pit of her stomach. She had made him angry by being so forward. Her face colored crimson as she realized what she had done. How could she have acted that way? She was normally painfully shy, yet with Decimus she felt like a flower beginning to newly bud, slowly opening to the world around it. Shaking her head, she turned and followed Candace to her own room.

Candace lit a lamp and pulled the draperies. Chara studied the room, awed by such wealth. Even her stepfather had not had such luxuries, and he had been a wealthy man.

When Candace left the room, Chara made ready for bed and slid between the silken sheets. She nestled snugly into the bedding, almost purring with contentment. She did not know what the future held for her, but she had learned to take one day at a time, and for now she would enjoy every moment of such luxurious living.

Closing her eyes, she began to pray. She didn't get far before tiredness overcame her and she drifted off into a dreamless sleep.

three

Decimus spent the next several days scouring the market-place for suitable clothing. Since the warm Mediterranean climate was predominant most of the year, and it was the middle of summer, only linen tunics were to be found.

He finally found what he was looking for at a little stall in a back alley near the docks. Placing his denarii on the counter, he rolled the wool tunics into a ball. Ever on the watch, he kept his eyes and ears open.

When he returned to the villa he found Chara waiting for him in the garden. "You found what you wanted?"

Decimus nodded. "Pretty much so. I still need to find fur-lined cloaks if possible. If not, we may have to wait until we reach Gaul to purchase them."

He laid the bundles on the bench beside her. "How are your feet this morning?"

Smiling, she held out one small foot, now encased in a leather sandal, for inspection. "Much better, as you can see. They are almost completely healed."

A half smile touched Decimus' lips. "It's fortunate that the first part of our journey will be by sea. You shouldn't have to do much walking." Moving the bundle of clothing aside, he sat down next to her. He twisted his fingers together, eyes focused on the ground. When he cleared his throat, Chara gazed at him expectantly.

"Is there. . .I mean do you. . ." He paused, turning slightly away from her. Picking up a dry flower petal from the ground he started crumbling it to pieces.

Chara waited, her soft brown eyes wandering over his features. He took his time before finally asking what was uppermost in his mind. "When we get to Gaul, is there anyone you wish to see?" His eyes found hers. "I mean is there family you wish to. . . ?"

Chara was already shaking her head. "There is no one. I have nowhere to go, if not with you."

Decimus considered her for a long time, then got up and started pacing in front of her. Running a hand in agitation through his hair, he came to an abrupt halt. Kneeling beside her, he tried to decide how he could explain certain things to her. She was such an innocent, she would probably have no idea what he was talking about.

"Chara. . ." Again he stopped. Before he could begin again, Antipus came into the garden.

"Well, hello. How did things go at the market today?"

Decimus sighed in relief. Perhaps Antipus would know a way to tell Chara the things that needed to be said. He would ask him later.

Decimus rose to his feet. "Things went well. I found most of what I needed."

"Probably cost you a few denarii, hmm?"

Grinning, Decimus confirmed it with a nod. "The old reprobate that sold me the woolen robes knew he had me in a tight spot. He was a smart old donkey."

Antipus laughed. "Probably Bacchus. He's the wiliest merchant in all of Rome. If you can't find what you are looking for anywhere else, Bacchus is sure to have it."

"Have you heard from Galla?" Decimus wanted to know.

Antipus turned an inquiring look on Chara and motioned to the bench where she was seated. "May I, my dear?" Smiling her consent, Chara moved to the side to allow Antipus to be seated. "No," he said, "he hasn't sent word to me."

Decimus sighed. "How long will it be, Antipus? The longer we stay, the better the chances of being caught and sent to the arena."

"Patience, my friend. Everything in good time. In the meantime, make yourself at home here. Agrippina and I welcome the diversion from our monotonous life."

"Your lady is a wonderful person," Chara told Antipus softly.

He smiled, touching Chara's cheek with his palm. "She certainly has fallen in love with you. She seems to think of you as the daughter we never had."

Chara didn't feel it her place to inquire, but her eyes held a question.

"No, child." Antipus told her. "Agrippina and I have no children of our own." Pain was in his eyes when he looked away. "It was just not to be. Now, well, now I thank God. Children would be just one more worry, more people for whose safety I would fear."

Thinking to deter the old man from his melancholy thoughts, Decimus pulled a small statue from his sack. He handed it to Antipus. "I found this at the market and thought that I would like you to have it. A small way of saying thank you."

Antipus held the statue cupped in his palms and his eyes filled with tears. A shepherd was carrying a lamb over his shoulder, his staff in his hands. Even such a small statue was intricately carved and detailed so that the man's features were clear. His chin was thrust forward in determination, yet his eyes were filled with joy. Decimus had marveled at it when he saw it at the idol merchant's stall. It was indeed a work of art.

"Just like our Lord," Antipus told them softly.

Decimus silently agreed. Those had been his same thoughts when he had spotted the shepherd among the other idols. When he looked at Chara her eyes were fixed intently on the statue. She glanced up at him and smiled, and Decimus caught his breath. When she smiled with her eyes like that, she was almost pretty.

Feeling foolish for such a flight of fancy, Decimus scowled and turned toward the villa. "There are some things I need to attend to before this evening." Bowing, he left them.

Chara followed him with her eyes. When he was out of sight, she turned back to Antipus. He was regarding her solemnly.

"You love him?"

Eyes wide, she would have denied it, but she wasn't sure that she could. "How can one tell after such a short time?" she remonstrated.

He smiled that gentle smile of his. "Agrippina and I knew the minute we laid eyes on each other. We were fortunate that our parents allowed us to marry, since we came from different backgrounds."

"You love her very much." It was a statement and not a question.

"Is that so surprising? We're old, but not yet dead. Agrippina is the other half of the clay that the Lord used to create me. I have never desired another."

Chara looked away. "I hope God has such a thing in store for me."

Antipus patted her hand. "He does, my dear, He does. So never settle for second best. You'll know if he's the right one. Sometimes people know right away, other times love grows slowly like the unfolding of a flower."

Getting up, Antipus waited for Chara to rise also. They made their way slowly back to the villa, and Chara thought how much she had grown to love this man and his wife in just the few days she had been here.

Agrippina met them in the atrium, smiling at her husband. "Beloved, can you spare me your charming companion?"

The elderly man arched a brow, cocking his head at Chara. He grinned, giving her a wink. "Well, if I must."

Agrippina's gaze followed her husband across the atrium. When she turned back to Chara, they still glowed with her love.

"I wondered if you would show me that intricate stitch you were telling me about. I have decided to use it to trim Antipus's tunic that I have had made for his birthday."

Chara smiled. "He'll be pleased."

While Agrippina was engrossed with her stitching, Chara took the time to study her. Her hair was piled on top of her head in an elaborate style that the Romans loved. Although it was streaked with gray, there was still much black showing through. Her face was unusually devoid of wrinkles for one of her age. Although Agrippina was slightly plump, she still had a fine figure for an older woman.

Chara longed to grow old with a husband of her own, but her stepbrother had pointed out to her time and time again that she had no looks and that no man would want her. She didn't want to believe him—but she did.

Candace knocked on the doorpost. "My lady, supper is ready."

Agrippina looked up in surprise. "Oh my goodness! Is it *that* late?" Apologetically she squeezed Chara's hand. "Oh my dear, I had no idea. And you just sat there patiently. Please forgive me."

When Chara and Agrippina descended the staircase, they were arm in arm laughing together. Decimus watched them from below and marveled again at how lovely Chara could look when she laughed. Her eyes lost their veiled look and took on a special radiance. Each time he saw her something seemed to tug at his heartstrings a little more. He shook his head in irritation. He was letting his imagination get away with him. Sara was the one he loved, the one he had longed for with every fiber of his being for years now. Hadn't he? Closing his eyes, he tried to picture her face, but no image came to mind except that of a young blond girl with artless brown eyes. Sara's hair had not been blond.

Decimus gritted his teeth in frustration. This was going to be a long journey and he needed to keep his wits about him. He surely didn't need his mind filled with confusing thoughts.

After the meal Antipus excused himself, saying that he needed to attend a party in honor of Senator Secubus. "Secubus is an old friend," he told them, lifting his mantle from the stool in the hallway. "It would seem odd if I didn't attend."

Agrippina folded her hands in front of her and gave her

husband a skeptical look. "Beloved, be careful."

He frowned at her. "I'm always careful, Agrippina. You know me."

"Yes, Antipus, I do. That's what causes my concern."

Decimus grinned as the old man threw his wife a disgusted look. After Agrippina closed the door behind him, Decimus stepped forward and put a hand on her arm. "My lady, could I have a word with you?"

Surprised, she glanced first at Chara. "Of course."

She followed him into the triclinium, where Decimus shut the doors carefully behind them.

Chara stared at the closed doors, knowing a moment's disquiet. What did Decimus wish to talk with Agrippina about? Was he going to suggest that she, Chara, remain in Rome after all? A knot formed in the pit of her stomach. Realizing that she could do nothing, she made her way to her room to prepare for the night.

A soft warm breeze stroked against her face as she stood leaning against the balcony. Turning her face into it, she closed her eyes, smiling with contentment. She had always loved the wind blowing against her face. Her mind turned to a Psalm of David that she had heard long ago, and she remembered that the psalmist had called the wind "God's breath." When the breeze drifted against her, she felt loved. Protected. If only she could always feel like that.

A noise from below indicated someone's presence. As she watched, Decimus came from the villa, his head bowed in thought. Chara watched him walk to the fountain and lean against it. His handsome face was creased with worry. What preyed so heavily on his mind?

Sensing someone watching him, Decimus turned and looked up. They stared at each other a long moment before Chara turned away.

When Decimus closed his eyes that night, a vision of Chara standing in the moonlight, her hair flowing like a golden halo around her head, filled his mind. He fervently hoped Agrippina could make Chara understand the things he couldn't bring himself to tell her.

๛

When Chara left Agrippina's room the next afternoon she was a wiser, if less naive, young lady. Her cheeks burned at the things Agrippina had shared with her. A young woman must always be aware that her actions can be misinterpreted by men; a young woman traveling alone with men is in a precarious position; a young woman in such a position must have extra care not to appear to be encouraging unwelcome advances. Had it been Decimus' idea to have Agrippina tell her all these things? She felt mortified. Was it because of the innocent kiss she had bestowed upon him that first night?

Chara's cheeks filled with color when she came upon Decimus in the atrium. His wide-eyed innocence convinced her, however, that he had had nothing to do with her enlightening conversation with Agrippina.

"You've been with Agrippina?"

Embarrassed, Chara looked away. "Yes. She had some things she wished to discuss with me."

"Indeed. I hope it was nothing too serious."

The color deepened in her cheeks. "No! No, not at all."

Decimus hid a grin. "Would you like to come with me to the market today? I have most of what we need for the journey, but there are some things that perhaps you need for yourself?"

Chara smiled brightly. "I would love to come. Let me tell Agrippina."

They wandered through the market, listening to the merchants hawk their wares. Everywhere the crowds surged around them, the clamor of different languages mixing together into a cacophony of sound. Decimus stopped at a booth and purchased two peaches. "Hungry?" he asked.

Chara shook her head. "No, but they look delicious."

"We'll save them for later."

As they meandered through the crowds, Chara began to feel happy. For a time she could forget that Rome hated Christians, she could forget that she was a slave, she could forget that her life was in danger. For a time she could pretend that she and Decimus were just a couple of. . .what?. . .friends?

"You were smiling a minute ago. Why the frown now?" Decimus demanded softly.

Chara looked away. "It's nothing." She stopped, eyes growing wide with fear. Decimus followed her look and encountered the eyes of the merchant who had bid against the priest at the market. The merchant's look roved boldly over Chara's form that in the past week had begun to fill out slightly.

Head thrown back in anger, Decimus glared at the man with cold blue eyes that glittered dangerously. Finally the man looked away, but not before throwing Decimus a murderous look.

"Let's go back to the villa," Chara begged softly. The afternoon had been ruined.

Decimus tilted her chin and her fears subsided at the calm look on his face. "You don't have to worry about men like that. I will let nothing happen to you. I promise."

She smiled wryly. "You shouldn't make promises you might not be able to keep."

He remained silent, knowing she was right. Taking her by the arm, he turned her in the opposite direction. "Maybe you're right. Maybe we should return to the villa."

Opening the gate that led to Antipus's villa, Decimus ushered Chara ahead of him. Once inside, they both seemed reluctant to part company. Instead, by unspoken consent, they wandered across the courtyard, pausing at last in front of the fountain.

Chara sat on the marble bench, but Decimus remained standing. He studied her face slowly, and Chara bent her head, embarrassed. Franco's critical words were never far from her thoughts. What did Decimus see when he looked at her? Was she only a responsibility to him? Seeing her reflection in the water, she knew it could not be otherwise.

"Hello."

Both Chara and Decimus glanced up, Chara smiling when she recognized Galla. He strode across the yard, motioning to the villa.

"I've been waiting to speak to you. You've been gone a long time." There was a question in his statement.

Bristling at the Roman's arrogance, Decimus took instant offense. This man didn't own him. At least not *yet*. "We were searching the market for any last-minute items we might need for the trip."

Galla's eyebrows flew up at the surly tone of voice. "It wasn't my intention to pry, or to suggest anything improper. I merely wondered if there had been some kind of trouble."

Feeling ashamed of his outburst of temper, Decimus shrugged. "Nothing important. We saw the merchant who was trying to buy Chara, but he didn't accost us in any way."

Galla's searching gaze flicked over Chara, but he could find no sign that she was upset or harmed in any way. Whatever had happened, the young Briton seemed to have taken care of the situation.

"I need to speak with you and Antipus. The time for our departure seems to be approaching more rapidly than I had anticipated."

Decimus gave him a questioning look but waited until Chara rose from her seat and followed them inside. A strained look about Galla's mouth didn't bode well for Decimus' peace of mind.

Antipus joined them in the triclinium, as did Agrippina. When they were all seated, Galla began to explain. "I'm not quite sure what has happened, but the army has ordered the search for Christians to be intensified." He looked at Antipus somberly. "It seems that it has come to the generals' attention that certain men within the Senate are following this 'vile sect,' as they call it."

The color drained from Agrippina's face. She reached her hand for her husband's. He clasped his fingers with hers and began to knead them gently. "Are there any names being mentioned?" he asked quietly.

"Some," Galla answered. "But not yours that I'm aware of."

The fear in the room seemed a tangible thing, leaving a sour taste in Chara's mouth. What were they to do now?

Galla rose. "There will be room for three others to go with us, but that's all I can arrange." He looked at Chara. "I'm afraid that I must insist that the others be all men. Anything else would be suspect."

Antipus nodded his head. "Agreed. I only wish. . ." He stopped, looking at his wife.

"Don't even think it," she told him firmly. "My place is with you, and I will not leave, no matter *what* you manage to arrange."

"Beloved."

Agrippina rose to her feet. "I will hear no more about it." Quickly she left the room.

Antipus was shaking his head. "She's a headstrong woman," he told them softly, "but what a woman."

Decimus felt the helplessness of the situation. "You have to leave, Antipus. It's no longer safe for you here."

The senator looked at him sadly. "Where would I go? I'm too old to be a missionary to Britannia. Besides, I may have nothing to fear. Whatever the circumstances, God will take care of me." He smiled at them. "And if it is my time to die, then no power on earth can stop it. Frankly, if not for Agrippina, I would be eager for death, for then I will see my Lord."

The room was silent. Galla and Decimus exchanged glances. Shrugging his shoulders, Decimus rose to his feet to stand beside Galla. "When will we leave?"

Galla sighed. "I'm still not sure, but you need to be prepared to leave at a moment's notice. Have your things packed and ready."

Antipus got to his feet. "I have something for you. Wait here."

He left the room and returned shortly with a large cedar box.

It had an inlaid mosaic design of pressed silver. Lifting the lid, Decimus could see that it was full of coins. Antipus lifted out a small bag and handed it to Galla.

"This is my contribution to your mission work in Britannia. Since I can't come myself, I want to have a part in spreading the Word."

Galla opened the bag curiously. His face paled and he glanced at Antipus in stunned disbelief. "There are several talents' worth of gold here!"

Antipus nodded. "One hundred to be precise."

Decimus' legs gave way and he dropped to the couch behind him. He was speechless. What a fortune!

Galla tried to hand the bag back to Antipus. "I can't take this. It's too much!"

"No. You have no idea what you will face when you reach Britannia. But one thing we know for certain, Roman currency is used there as well as everywhere else." Pushing Galla's hand away, Antipus smiled at him. "You have no idea where you will be able to find work or how you can make a living. Take it." He smiled at Decimus. "It's for all of you, including Chara and the other three men that I will choose to send with you."

Galla's voice was hoarse as he gave Antipus his sincere thanks. He handed the bag to Decimus. "You take care of it. I have to return to the garrison and then to the palace. I must keep my eyes and ears open." His look was intent. "Remember, have your things ready."

Decimus felt a cold finger of foreboding slide down his spine. "I'll see to it right away."

Galla nodded. Turning, he gave Chara a half-smile before he rapidly exited the room.

Antipus watched him go. He stood staring after him for several moments before he turned back to Decimus and Chara. "I must go see to Agrippina."

After he left the room, Decimus slowly rose to his feet again, taking a deep breath and releasing it slowly. He turned to Chara. "We need to get our things together."

She didn't answer right away. When she finally looked at him again there were tears in her eyes. "What of Antipus and Agrippina?"

Pressing his lips together, he avoided her eyes. "I don't know. All we can do is pray."

"Can't we. . ."

"No," he interrupted angrily. "We cannot *force* someone to do something they don't wish to do. In the end, we are all responsible for our own actions."

A tear trickled down Chara's cheek and she rose slowly to her feet. "I'll see to the packing."

Decimus noticed the tear and felt his own frustrations mount. Why was God letting all of this happen to the people who loved Him most? Why were such evil men allowed to live and prosper and yet the obedient suffered? He had no answer.

He wanted to reach out and take Chara into his arms and soothe away her hurt, but how could he when he didn't know how to make it right? What words of comfort could he offer when he had so many questions of his own?

He watched as Chara walked out of the room, her head bowed low. Sighing, he clenched the bag of coins. A veritable fortune. But what good was money if you died before you could use it? Tucking the bag into his belt, he followed Chara from the room.

four

That evening Antipus had three guests for supper. Each man was a Christian, and each had his own story to tell.

Caleb was a slave of Judea who had been in hiding for some time, ever since his master had been killed in an accident involving a chariot. Caleb was a Jew, but a converted Jew who now served the Lord Jesus, and when the opportunity had presented itself, Caleb fled to other Christians who were willing to hide him until they could conceive of a way to get him out of Rome. Although the authorities weren't looking for him, per se, they were always on the watch for runaways. Especially someone who would prove useful in the arenas.

Caleb hated his slavery, but he had felt compelled to serve his master well, since the Apostle Paul had commanded it. But upon the death of his master, Caleb had fled. Since the one who owned him was now dead, Caleb was not waiting around for someone else to take his place. He had done his duty, and now he considered himself free.

Then there was Thomas, a Greek. He had been set free from slavery years before when he had saved from drowning the little girl of his master. Since she was an only child and dearly beloved, they had repaid him with his freedom.

He had remained with the family as a servant, doing what they had purchased him to do, teaching their children Greek and Greek literature. Thomas was a very learned man, a man of letters.

And last, but not least, was Trophimus, a very young Roman who had recently witnessed his parents' death in the arena. Although Trophimus's father had been an influential man, not even that had been able to save him when it was discovered that he was a member of the Christian sect.

Chara felt drawn to the young boy. He couldn't have been as old as her own eighteen years of age, and he seemed even younger than his chronological age. She smiled gently when she was introduced and felt a decidedly motherly urge to protect him.

As they dined on pheasant and fish from the Mediterranean, they got to know one another. Antipus explained Galla's plan for getting them out of the city.

Caleb's dark eyes flashed. "You expect me to sell myself to a Roman? Willingly?" He rose to his feet, and Chara noticed the man's powerful build. Although he was probably middle-aged, he was a commanding presence. "Never!"

Antipus frowned, motioning for him to be seated again. "Galla is a Christian, and although he feels slavery to be wrong, still he is willing to purchase all of you for a short period of time."

"How kind!" Thomas's voice dripped with sarcasm.

Antipus sighed. "Let me try to explain this better. Galla being a Christian will not lie. Now, if you are going to accompany him on this trip, you will need to be just what he says you are. His slaves. If you have a problem with this, let me know now and I will arrange for someone else to take your place. God knows, there are enough Christians willing to leave Rome."

"But a Roman? How do we know it's not a trick? How do we know we can trust him?" Caleb was clearly unconvinced.

Trophimus spoke quietly. "Antipus is a Roman, too. What matter if he be Roman or not? In Christ, aren't we all the same? This is what my father taught me." He glared at Caleb, but there were tears in his eyes. "Unless my father died for nothing."

The room grew quiet and each member felt convicted by the young man's words. Clearing his throat, Antipus rose to his feet. "I have made arrangements for Caleb and Trophimus to remain here. You will be safe, and we can easily locate you in case we have to expedite things. Thomas, we know where to locate you, but we must know of your whereabouts at all times. If you are called upon to leave in a hurry we don't want to have to leave someone behind." His warning was clear.

After the meal, everyone separated to their assigned rooms. Murmured conversations could be heard as they ascended the stairs, the fear evident in their quiet voices.

As Chara was about to go upstairs, Decimus placed a restraining hand on her arm. "I need to talk to you a moment. In the peristyle."

Surprised, she followed him out into the garden. He had taken great pains to avoid being alone with her lately, and she wondered at his motives now. Still, she followed him to the bench and seated herself, staring up at his pensive face.

Decimus cleared his throat. It was important to him that he make her understand his position, and where she stood in all of this chaos. "Chara, you know that I don't wish for you to remain a slave." He stopped when her head dropped forward, blond hair hiding her face from view. What was she thinking? In the short time he had come to know her, he realized that this woman was completely devoid of conceit. She was lacking in confidence in herself, or anything about herself. He knew that if he said the wrong thing, she would retreat inside herself where he would have trouble reaching her.

"I hope you will understand when I tell you that I cannot give you your freedom just yet."

Her eyes flew to his face, but she remained silent.

"When I. . ." He paused, finding it hard to utter the words. "When I sell myself to Galla, everything that I own becomes his by right of possession." He watched her face closely. "That includes you."

Wrinkling her forehead, she spoke for the first time. "I don't understand. What are you trying to say?"

"Galla decided it would be easier all around if I retained possession of you instead of giving you your freedom before he purchased it back. He thinks that this would be the best way in case anything happens to him."

Chara smiled. "If he thinks it best, then I have no qualms. I trust Galla completely."

Decimus frowned. She was so frustratingly innocent. Although he liked the Roman, he still wasn't sure he trusted him completely.

"He will *own* you."

"As you own me now?"

Decimus brushed his hand through his hair in exasperation. How could he make her see? "That's different."

"How so?" She looked at him skeptically and he had to refrain from gritting his teeth.

"He. . .I. . .there's a difference."

"I don't see how." Rising to her feet, she laid a hand against his arm. "I understand your feelings, but I trust Galla. He's done nothing to prove otherwise."

Decimus sighed. "I don't want to see you hurt, or anything to happen to you. I have considered you my own responsibility for some time now. It will be hard for me to relinquish that chore to someone else."

He could feel her withdraw from him even though she made no movement. Her eyes grew distant. Now what had he said? Every time he talked to the girl he felt he was treading on eggshells.

"Have no fear," she told him angrily. "Whether owned by you, or someone else, I will obey." Turning, she hastened across the garden.

"Chara!"

She froze at the command in his voice. He walked up behind her. His hands moved as though to reach for her shoulders, but he didn't touch her.

She refused to look at him. "May I go now? I have things to attend to."

Sighing, Decimus dropped his hands to his sides. "Yes, you may go." He watched her walk away, her head bent low. Raising his eyes heavenward, he threw up a petition on her behalf and then one for himself and then while he was at it, for them all.

༈

Three days later Chara and Candace were crossing the hallway when a furious pounding shook the door. They exchanged fearful glances before Candace slowly went to the door and opened it just a crack. She fell backwards as Galla pushed his way in.

"Where's Decimus?"

Chara felt her heart drop. Galla spotted her and came quickly to her side. "Get your things. I have to get you out of here."

"What's happened?"

"They arrested Antipus today. Where's Agrippina?"

Fear clutched Chara's insides. "She went to the market-place."

He grit his teeth with frustration. Raking his fingers through his dark hair, he fixed his eyes intensely on Chara. "Get the others. We have to move you now."

"But what of Agrippina?"

He shook her slightly. "Get the others!"

Conditioned to obey, Chara fled upstairs. Galla followed her with his eyes before turning to Candace still clutching the door. "Tell the other servants. Antipus has been arrested."

Eyes wide with fear, Candace turned to obey. She turned back, tears in her eyes. "What will happen to him?"

Galla pressed his lips together. "I don't know, but it doesn't look good. Nero's generals have never particularly liked Antipus. Antipus is too pure a man in Nero's debauched empire. He shows Nero up for the depraved lunatic that he is."

Candace hastened away to tell the others. Galla knew that Antipus had given each of the servants money just in case such an event would happen. Pray God they would find places of refuge.

Decimus came quickly down the stairs to meet him. "Chara said that Antipus has been arrested?"

Galla nodded. "I have to move you to a different location.

Thomas will be safe for the time being, but soldiers will be here, probably within the hour."

"We're ready. Caleb and Trophimus are getting their things and then we will be ready to leave. Where will you take us?"

"A man who lives close to the docks is a Christian sympathizer. He will hide you in one of his warehouses until I can make different arrangements." Galla glanced around him. "It won't be as comfortable as this, but it should be safe. Right now the soldiers are searching only private residences. It hasn't occurred to them to look in the storehouses and such."

"Thank God for that!" Decimus turned as Chara hurried down the steps. She had a large bundle clutched in her hands.

"Is this all you have?" Galla wanted to know.

Decimus nodded. "I thought it best if we have only what we could use. We can purchase other things as we have need of them."

Trophimus came down the stairs followed by Caleb, each carrying a bundle. A faint raise of Caleb's eyebrows asked the question they all wanted to ask.

"There's a wagon at the back gate," he told them. "You will be taken to your new hiding place." Galla stared intently at each one. "Remember, each one of your lives is dependent on your cooperation with each other."

Galla let the warning sink in before ushering them out to the courtyard and through the gate. A wagon was sitting there, almost filled with baskets of grain. Galla opened one basket that was empty and motioned for Chara to get in. Decimus lifted her to the wagon and helped her inside.

Each person in turn got into one of the baskets, all except Decimus.

"You will be the driver." Galla gave Decimus instructions on where to find the storehouses and told him to ask for a man named Aureus. "He'll take it from there. God go with you."

Decimus climbed into the wagon. Lifting the reins, he turned to Galla and they stared at each other a long time.

"God keep you safe," Decimus told him.

"And you," Galla answered softly.

When Decimus reached the warehouse he had no trouble locating Aureus. The docks were a bubbling hive of activity. Merchants hastened to and fro, checking on the progress of their imports and exports. People were everywhere, yet no one seemed to take particular notice of the wagon and its driver.

Aureus met Decimus at the door to one of warehouses, opening wide the portal and motioning Decimus inside. Pulling the door closed after him, he met Decimus at the back of the wagon. Together they opened each basket and helped its occupant to alight.

Aureus's eyes opened wide at the sight of Chara, her blond hair swinging around her shoulders as she climbed down from the wagon.

"A woman?" he questioned.

Decimus didn't answer him. "Where do we go from here?"

Dragging his gaze from Chara, the old man motioned toward the back of the storehouse. "This way. It isn't much, but you should be safe here. At least until Galla makes arrangements otherwise."

They followed him through the semidarkness, their eyes slowly adjusting to the dimness. Although Aureus looked elderly, his spry movements gave the impression of a much younger man. His head was bald on top with a curl of white ringing the edges. When he smiled, his teeth were yellow and a few were missing.

"You'll have to make arrangements between you on what to do with the young lady. There will be little privacy here."

Chara colored hotly, remembering her conversation with Agrippina.

"We will manage something," Decimus told the man, not unaware of Chara's embarrassment.

Nodding his head, Aureus turned to leave. "There are provisions over there." He motioned to a corner where several baskets and chests were stacked. "Help yourselves. I'll try to stop by daily to see if you need anything."

"How long?" Caleb didn't appreciate the tomblike darkness and stuffy atmosphere, though he knew he could survive anything as long as it wasn't for an extended period of time.

Aureus continued on his way, shrugging his shoulders. "Don't know. You'll have to wait for Galla."

They heard the door slide closed behind Aureus as he exited. Decimus turned to the others. "Well, let's see what we have here."

They opened baskets and chests and found, among other things, bed linen and pillows. Decimus looked around him, trying to figure some way to afford Chara some privacy. Taking one of the blankets, he arranged it between some stacked crates of goods, improvising a small room.

He grinned at her. "Your quarters, my lady."

Smiling, Chara thanked him and lay her bundle down in the rough shelter. It wasn't much, but his thoughtfulness pleased her.

Trophimus dropped his own bundle in the corner. Crossing his legs at the ankles, he lowered himself to the ground. He leaned back against the wall and closed his eyes.

Decimus watched Caleb do the same. He wondered how long they would all have to stay here, but more than that he wondered what was happening to Antipus and Agrippina.

He looked behind the blanket barrier he had constructed for Chara and found her on her knees, her lips moving rapidly in silence. Going over, he dropped down beside her and took her hand in his. She glanced up in surprise.

"I thought I would join you, if you don't mind."

Giving him a half-smile, she bowed her head again.

‰

Galla listened to the conversations going on around him, all the while trying to see into the senate chambers. He could hear the loud discussions, but couldn't see any of the speakers. Frustrated, he pushed his way forward.

"Senator Secubus, we all know that you and Senator Antipus are close friends. Perhaps you share this odious religion of his?"

There was a threat hanging in the words.

"I have always been loyal to Rome! How dare you, Fendicus, try to trap me in this same vile net you have managed to spread out to others." Secubus's angry voice reached clearly into the hall. "Perhaps you have something yourself to hide."

Instead of being angry, Fendicus's voice was low and compelling. "You can't transfer suspicion to me, my friend. *I* am not the one helping Christians to flee Rome."

"And you think Antipus is?"

"We have proof," another voice intoned.

There was silence for a full minute. "What proof have you, Trinian? The word of a beaten slave?"

"No, Secubus. The word of a perfectly healthy, but *loyal,* servant of Rome. A servant in Antipus's own home."

Galla gasped softly. Someone in Antipus's house was a traitor and had informed the government of Antipus's activities. Galla leaned weakly against the wall, closing his eyes. What had he done? He should never have invited Antipus to be a part of his clandestine activities.

His eyes flew open. Did they then know of his own part in these proceedings? If not, they surely would soon. Who was the informer? Galla felt a murderous rage well up inside him. A good man might possibly die because of someone else's perfidy.

Turning, he quickly forced his way through the press of people and headed for the street. He hadn't much time. He had to act quickly.

❧

It was dark when the door slid open again. The stillness on the docks compared to that of the activity this morning was disquieting. The refugees remained absolutely immobile until they recognized a whispered voice.

"Decimus?"

"Here." Decimus made his way to Galla's side. "What news?"

Galla shook his head solemnly. "It's not good I'm afraid. There was a spy in Antipus's house."

A soft gasp caused both men to spin quickly around. Chara stood silhouetted in the moonlight from outside. Decimus took her arm and quickly moved her aside.

"My lady?" she queried softly.

Galla shook his head. "I don't know."

"What do we do now?" Decimus wanted to know. "We can't stay here. Surely they must know about you."

"I'm not sure if they do, but you're right. There's always that chance." He lifted the papers he held in his hands. "I've brought the papers to make the purchase of the three of you as slaves." He looked at Chara. "Has he explained about you?"

Chara nodded. "If anything happens to you, I will still be his *responsibility*."

Galla's eyebrows raised slightly at her surly tone of voice, and he glanced at Decimus, who merely shrugged his shoulders. Who knew what went on in the minds of women?

Galla followed them to the back of the shelter and nodded to Trophimus and Caleb. "I've sent word to Thomas. He should be here soon. Right now, let's get on with business and I will explain my plans."

When the arrangements were finalized, Galla took the papers and carefully rolled them up. Placing them inside his breastplate, he then motioned for them all to be seated. Before he could explain, the door to the outside opened again. Galla doused the lamp and everyone became still.

Soft footsteps came hesitantly toward them, stopping periodically. "Is anyone here?"

Decimus sighed with relief. "Thomas."

Thomas joined the group, clutching a bundle. Galla proceeded to explain the events of the afternoon to him, and Thomas nodded sadly. "I know. I heard from one of the servants that Agrippina had been taken into custody also."

"Do you know where they are being held?"

Thomas hesitated so long Decimus thought he wasn't

going to answer. He nodded slowly. "They are in the dungeons below the arena."

"Dear God!" Chara buried her face in her hands.

"What can we do?" Decimus wanted to know.

"There's nothing we can do." Galla's quiet voice brought Caleb to his feet.

"We have to do something! We can't just let them die!"

"Will it help Antipus if we all die? Would that make him happy?" Galla was angry, not only with Caleb but with himself. He felt impotent, unable to do anything. As a trained soldier of Rome he found this unacceptable and frustrating.

"Is there nothing we can do?"

Galla stared grimly at Chara's tear-streaked face. "Pray."

"What will *you* do now?" Decimus wanted to know.

Galla turned away. "I have to return to the garrison. I will make arrangements to sail two days from now."

"What if they arrest you also? What if they know that you've been helping Antipus?" Decimus had no idea what would become of them if the soldier were taken also. He felt his frustrations begin to mount.

"Aureus will try to find a way to get you on board a ship going somewhere. You still have the money Antipus gave us?"

Decimus swallowed a knot in this throat. "Yes."

Galla nodded, then quickly turned and left.

"Two days." Trophimus sighed. "Better get some sleep while we can. Who knows what the morrow will bring."

"God knows, Trophimus." Chara told him. "If He cares enough to know the number of hairs on your head, then He is concerned with your whole life."

Trophimus smiled weakly. "I know that in my heart, but sometimes my head gets in my way."

"You're not alone," Thomas told him, sitting next to him. "I, too, struggle with doubts when a good man like Antipus suffers and an evil one like Nero doesn't."

"You forget," Chara told them. "Antipus's suffering will

only last a short time, but Nero's an eternity unless he repents his wickedness."

Decimus marveled at her faith. How had she come by it? In Gaul, of all places. How had she learned of Jesus when she lived so far from the Judean realm? He would ask her sometime, but right now she looked exhausted.

Decimus helped Chara to her feet and led her to the cubbyhole they had made earlier. He looked long into her face, his eyes tracing the paths her tears had left on her cheeks. She looked so little, so helpless. Without giving it any thought, he pulled her gently into his arms and held her close. He could feel her sobs begin again.

"We'll be all right," he told her softly.

Her voice came back to him, muffled by his tunic. "But what of them?"

He knew to whom she was referring. "I don't know. We'll have to wait and see."

He held her close a moment longer, then gently pushed her away. "Try to get some sleep."

Nodding, she turned away from him, pulling the blanket closed behind her.

five

When Galla joined them at the docks two days later, his face looked haggard, his mouth tight. Decimus knew something was terribly wrong, but Chara was the one who asked the question they were all afraid to say.

"Any news?" Her soft voice trembled slightly.

His gaze went to Decimus, who read the grim message there. Moving closer to Chara, Decimus placed an arm around her shoulders.

"Antipus and Agrippina were sent to the arena yesterday with about thirty others."

Chara felt her legs give way beneath her. Thankful for Decimus' support, she leaned against him, and he lifted her in his arms and strode to her cubbyhole, laying her gently on the blanket. Chara turned her face against the bedding, her sobbing echoing eerily in the warehouse.

Decimus joined the others. "What now?"

"I've arranged passage for tomorrow. Myself and five slaves. When I get here tomorrow, be ready to attach yourselves to my retinue. Make it seem as though you are entering the docks with me."

They all nodded in agreement. Decimus considered the Roman a moment, noticing that for all his strength his muscles were shaking. Was he as afraid as the rest of them? Or was he worried about something else?

"Was your name implicated with the others?"

Galla shook his head. "No, and since it wasn't, I have a pretty good idea of who the perpetrator was. Antipus mentioned that one of his menservants was visiting family these last few weeks. Undoubtedly, the scoundrel wanted to be out of the house before he went to the emperor's generals with his betrayal, and his story about his family was just that—a story. Because he was not there these last weeks, he did not find out about my connection with Antipus. Or yours. I hope his guilt rests heavily on his shoulders." Galla's eyes gleamed, and Decimus wondered if he was considering retribution.

"I'll leave you now. Be ready when I return on the morrow." He turned away but then turned back. His eyes went to the corner where quiet sobs could still be heard. "Will she be all right?"

Decimus followed his look. His heart went out to Chara for she had really loved the old man and his wife. They had treated her as a beloved child. "Only time will heal such wounds."

Glancing back at Decimus, Galla nodded his head. He walked out the door and gently closed it behind him.

"I hope he wasn't followed." Caleb's voice was tense.

"Why should he be? He said he wasn't suspected." Thomas turned away and went and sat near Chara's cubicle. Trophimus followed him, his eyes flicking toward Chara's blanket and then away.

"I could go crazy cooped up in here." Caleb grabbed an orange and began to peel it.

"Better here than in the dungeons below the arena," Decimus told him roughly.

The hours seemed to drag by. Periodically Caleb would get up and begin to pace. His constant restlessness was beginning to wear on Decimus' already tattered nerves.

Darkness descended and still nothing happened. Chara remained quietly in her cubicle until hunger drew her forth. The others watched her discreetly as she found some dates and began to chew them. Decimus rose and went to her.

"Are you all right?" he asked her softly, noticing her swollen, red eyes.

She nodded her head slightly before lifting her eyes to his. The pain he saw there mirrored his own. "Why couldn't they have come with us? Why?" She looked at him without really seeing him. "Antipus will never see the beautiful robe Agrippina was making for him."

Turning, she went back to her pallet and lay down. Closing her eyes, she tried to sleep.

Decimus found it impossible to sleep himself. Finding a comfortable position next to the door, he decided to keep watch. They had to be ready when Galla returned.

The moon rose golden and full, a lover's moon. Decimus smiled wryly. The moon was just the same as the night he had left Antonius's villa. And Sara.

Closing his eyes, he leaned his head back against the wall. He should never have left Ephesus. Instead of solving his problems, it had escalated them.

At times he longed for the days when he had served in the house of Antonius, for though he had been their slave, he had been happy with Diana and her family. In his heart, Antonius's sister had become the sister he had left behind in Britannia. He missed Diana as much as he had missed Sara.

He frowned. *Had* missed? Did he not miss Sara now? Where were the feelings he had thought were so intense? Now when he remembered Sara, he remembered more the things she had said than the way she looked. He could remember one time when they had sat and discussed the Scriptures, arguing the finer points of the Law. As a Jew, Sara knew so much more about the Scriptures than he had. Always, Sara had put God's will before her own.

Faint fingers of vermilion were creeping across the pre-dawn sky when Decimus roused the others. Quickly gathering their things together, they waited and watched from the door for Galla's arrival. The docks were soon brimming with activity. With so many people, they should be able to blend in easily.

Before long they spotted Galla wending his way through the crowds of people. He was followed by four wagons and several servants carrying loads of goods. When he drew close to the warehouse, Decimus and the others slipped in among the wagons, following Galla as he headed for a large cargo ship at the end of the pier.

Normally cargo ships allowed many passengers to travel on their open decks, but this particular ship showed no signs of such activity. A Roman soldier strode down the dropped plank to meet Galla as he came to a stop. "Centurion." He nodded.

"You have made room for my goods and slaves?" Galla's voice betrayed none of his trepidation. Now he would know if his name had been implicated with the others.

The soldier looked around at the array of wagons and servants. His eyebrows rose. "I was told there would be *five* slaves."

"As there are. These other servants are here merely to help load the trade goods meant for Britannia."

The soldier looked at everything carefully before tipping his head. "Your quarters have been arranged. Your slaves can find room on the deck."

Galla motioned to those standing near. "Start loading." He turned to the soldier. "Show them where to stow these things."

"Aye, centurion." Slapping a fist against his chest in salute, he turned and preceded them up the gangplank.

When they reached the deck, Chara stayed close to Decimus to avoid being trampled by the hurrying sailors as they scurried to their tasks. Everywhere was pandemonium, yet there was purpose in each sailor's face and order in the way they proceeded. Obviously, they knew what they were about.

Galla froze as several soldiers came up the steps from below ship. "What are they doing here?" Decimus whispered.

"I have no idea, but I'm about to find out."

He crossed the deck quickly, and Chara leaned closer to Decimus. Without thinking, he put his arm around her. They waited in silence until Galla returned.

"They have been sent to help guard the ship from pirates. Apparently, the raidings on the seas have increased, and Nero's army is determined that these supplies get to their troops in Britannia. It seems Roman spies have heard word of another Briton uprising brewing." He rubbed his chin thoughtfully. "I've wondered why General Agabus was so anxious to help me reach Britannia. *Trade goods,* he said."

"You think he has an ulterior motive?" Decimus inquired.

"I do now," Galla answered him calmly. "I'm afraid we're faced with another problem right now, though."

Decimus waited for him to elucidate.

Galla's eyes were probing the ship and its occupants. His look settled on Chara. "Have you noticed there are no other women?"

Surprised, Decimus and Chara looked around at the hubbub of activity. Decimus and Galla exchanged glances.

"What do we do? Will there be no other female passengers?"

Galla shook his head. "Every nook and cranny is being used to store supplies going to Britannia. And then there's the soldiers as well."

"How many soldiers are there?" Decimus was beginning to feel strangely uneasy.

"Only about twenty. They needed to save the room for the supplies. It looks like they're planning for a campaign, though, and somehow I have become a part of it. General Agabus probably didn't think that I would be bringing a woman, and since she's a slave I doubt he would have cared anyway."

Chara glanced up at Decimus, worrying her bottom lip with her teeth. Decimus sighed. "What do we do now?"

"Chara will have to stay in my quarters."

Decimus felt heat surge through his body at the suggestion. Noticing the ominous gleam in the young Briton's eyes, Galla shrugged. "It's the only way to protect her. Look around you."

Decimus looked. Many of the sailors and soldiers had stopped to stare at Chara. Some were nudging others, their whispers and ribald laughter reaching across the distance. Decimus felt the heat in his body intensify. Helplessness again caused his temper to flare.

Galla's lips pressed tightly together. "You had better get a grip on your jealous possessiveness, Decimus. I won't have you jeopardizing our plans." Taking Chara's arm, he propelled her across the deck and below.

Decimus watched their progress, stunned at Galla's assessment of the situation. Was he jealous? Ridiculous! One had to really care for someone to be jealous of them. He cared about Chara, but not *that* way. Deciding that the Roman was imagining things, Decimus went to find the others.

ta

Three days at sea, and still the beautiful weather held. Chara lifted her face to the salty breeze and smiled with contentment. Free from Rome, at least for the most part. She looked around her, watching several of the Roman soldiers lolling about on the decks. Many eyes turned her way and Chara shivered.

Decimus joined her at the rail, a half-smile curving his lips. "You look well."

Chara returned his smile. "I am."

"No seasickness?"

She grinned. "None. I wish I could say the same for poor Trophimus."

Decimus turned his head in the direction of the young Roman. Trophimus had spent the better part of the last three days hanging his head over the side of the ship. Decimus smiled in sympathy when the young boy slowly made his way across deck and dropped down on his pallet.

He turned his eyes back to Chara. He was hesitant to ask her anything about the sleeping arrangements that had been made between her and Galla, but he had to know.

"You and Galla. . ." He could not think how to phrase his

question.

Chara glanced at him and then away, refusing to say anything unless he specifically asked.

Decimus cleared his throat. "Things are well?"

Taking pity on his obvious distress, Chara looked him full in the face. Her soft brown eyes hardened perceptibly. "Galla treats me as a sister. He has given me the bunk in his cabin and he sleeps on the floor by the door."

Decimus looked away, embarrassed. "He protects you well." He felt aggravated that he was not the one watching out for Chara. After all, didn't she belong to him? He caught his thoughts up short. What was he thinking? He didn't own the girl. Not really. No one could really own another person, especially one who already belonged to God.

Decimus stared at a dolphin in the distance. "How do you come to know so much about Christianity?"

Blinking her eyes, Chara needed a moment to collect her thoughts after such an abrupt change of subject. She followed his look, smiling at the dolphin who was shortly joined by others.

"My mother taught me."

Decimus raised an eyebrow quizzically. "And how did she know so much? Gaul is a long way from Judea."

"My mother was a young girl living in Galilee at the time Christ was there."

Decimus' eyes widened. "Did she actually get to see Him?"

Chara nodded. "He spoke to the multitudes of which she was one. She was only seventeen at the time and a slave in the house of a Roman official. She went to hear Him speak one day. She realized there was something different about Him. She said He spoke with such power and authority one couldn't help but believe Him."

"What did He speak about?" Decimus asked curiously.

"Love, mainly. Loving each other and *especially* loving God."

"But at that time, Jesus preached only to the Jews. How came your mother to hear Him?"

Chara shook her head. "No, He spoke to the crowd. Many among the crowd were Gentiles. Perhaps He *was* only speaking to the Jews, but many others heard Him also."

Decimus glanced back to sea, his blond hair tossed in the breeze. "I wish I could have heard Him."

Chara agreed. How wonderful to have actually heard the voice of the Master, to have actually seen His face. She turned to Decimus and smiled. "True, that would have been wonderful, but thank God we now have the message of salvation as well as the Jews."

Decimus returned her smile. Reaching up a hand he pushed her hair behind her shoulder, letting his hand slide down her arm.

"What goes on here?"

Decimus and Chara jumped. The Roman soldier who had saluted Galla stood behind them, glaring at them. His coldly gleaming eyes went over Chara's flushed countenance. "You there, you dare to dally with your master's slave? He'll have you horsewhipped." His eyes went boldly down Chara's slender form. "I can't blame you, mind. But the centurion is not one to take an infraction lightly."

As the soldier's eyes continued their inspection, Decimus' hands curled at his side. He took a step forward, but Chara quickly placed a hand on his arm.

"We were doing nothing wrong."

"I'll bet," he sneered contemptuously and Decimus had the urge to strike him. Unconsciously, he stepped forward. Suddenly he was jerked around. Surprised, he came face to face with Galla.

"Is there a problem?" Galla asked softly. No one was fooled by the quietness of his voice, least of all the Roman soldier.

Snapping a salute, the soldier motioned to Decimus and Chara. "I found them together. The man seemed to be making free with his hands."

Galla turned to Decimus, his eyebrows going upwards. Decimus felt himself flush with hot color, embarrassed and angry.

"We were doing nothing, my lord, except talking," Chara told him quietly.

"Go to our quarters," Galla told her. She looked from one to the other, then hastily did as he commanded. Decimus felt himself growing angrier by the minute.

Lifting his hand, Galla struck Decimus a blow across the face that sent the young man reeling. He turned an accusing face toward Galla, who motioned his head slightly to his left. Decimus looked that way, surprised to see several Roman soldiers standing there. Understanding dawned and Decimus dropped his eyes.

"I will speak with you about this later. Go below and make yourself useful."

Galla watched Decimus walk away and hoped that he understood why he had done what he did. Galla couldn't afford to lose the respect of these Roman soldiers. He and the others had a lot at stake here. He turned to the men. "Be about your business."

They quickly dispersed and Galla went to his quarters.

After that, Decimus was careful to keep his distance from Chara, although whenever she was on deck, Galla made a point to be with her. For the most part she remained in the cabin, safely out of sight.

The weather changed as they grew closer to Gaul. The winds increased and the sea grew choppy. Trophimus, who had recovered from his seasickness, once again took to the rails.

Galla found Decimus unlacing the ropes from the sails. Bending down, Galla gave him a hand.

"I haven't had time to apologize for the other day—nor to explain." He kept his voice soft for fear of being overheard.

Decimus continued his work without looking up. "Not necessary." He rolled the sails, lashing them tightly in place.

Finally he looked at Galla and smiled slightly. "I've always had a rather violent temper."

Galla smiled back, relieved that Decimus showed him no ill will. Decimus rose to his feet. "My temper is something the Lord and I are working to change." His voice was barely louder than a whisper.

Galla rose also and said in an equally soft voice, "Sometimes a temper is not such a bad thing. Many a battle has been won by sheer anger. I—"

A shout interrupted his words. "Ship on the horizon!"

Turning in the direction the lookout indicated, men scurried to the rails, straining their eyes to see.

"Can you make anything out?" the captain wanted to know.

"I can't tell yet," the lookout hollered back down. "It's still too far."

Tension mounted as the ship drew closer. Finally the lookout yelled to the captain. "Pirates!"

There was instant pandemonium. The captain gave the orders to raise the sails again and the sailors jumped to obey.

"What are you going to do?" Galla asked the captain, his attention focused on the rapidly approaching ship.

"We're too loaded down to outrun them without the wind at our backs. We'll have to try to go with the wind."

"That will take us off course."

"It's the only chance we have," the captain told him grimly.

"Turn starboard!" the captain yelled and Decimus could feel the instant change in the movement of the ship. "Set sails!"

The sails billowed out instantly, filled with the strong wind. They were now headed off course at a rapid rate, and yet still the pirate ship gained on them, little by little.

"Arm yourself!" Galla commanded and the soldiers hastened to obey. They quickly gathered swords and javelins and took positions on the port side of the ship.

The pirate ship was close enough for Decimus to make out individual figures on the decks. He counted at least fifty men. The Roman ship was outnumbered, he realized, but not badly.

Decimus noticed Chara among the men lining the rails. Quickly, he crossed to her side. Taking her by the arm, he hurried her down the steps to Galla's quarters. "Stay here!" he commanded, and his voice brooked no argument.

Chara sank to the bunk, listening to feet pounding above her head. What was happening up there? Could they withstand an attack? Sliding quickly to her knees she began to fervently pray.

At the rails, Galla watched intensely as the ship drew closer. He prayed to God that his people would be kept safe. What irony to flee death sentences in Rome only to meet their deaths at the hands of pirates. He knew his men were strong and competent and might win the day, but *someone* was bound to die in the skirmish. He prayed that Chara would be spared.

A fiery arrow flew across the water, falling short of its intended target. Others followed, arriving closer each time.

Decimus gritted his teeth as he prepared to defend himself. He had never been trained in the arts of self-defense and he knew less about using weaponry, but he wielded his sword with a determination that surprised Galla.

Suddenly the pirate ship veered off. The Roman ship's occupants hurried to the port side as the pirate ship put distance between them.

"What happened?" Decimus asked Galla under cover of the confusion.

"I don't know!" He was as confounded as the rest of them.

"Ship off the starboard!"

All eyes turned in time to see a Roman triple-banked warship slide around from their left. Its three rows of oars sliced effortlessly through the water, adding momentum to the wind that suddenly filled their sail.

The Roman warship rapidly cut the distance between itself

and the pirate ship. As it drew closer, Decimus could see the soldiers as they prepared for battle. The pirate ship was hopelessly outnumbered.

Before long the warship overtook the other. Their speed had been rapid and they were so far away by this time that Decimus could barely see the figures of men running to and fro. A plank was dropped from the Roman ship to the pirates', and troops surged across.

"Poor lost devils," Galla commented softly.

Decimus watched as fire filled the sails of the pirate ship. The battle was over almost before it had begun.

"Drop sails!" the captain bellowed. "Man the oars!"

The ship moved sluggishly against the wind. Before long they were back on course.

Decimus went to Galla's cabin and found Chara curled up in a ball on the bunk. Her eyes were frightened and her lip trembled noticeably. She was clutching Galla's dagger in her hands.

Decimus' lips twitched. "Are you going to use that on me?"

Giving a sharp cry, she threw the dagger to the bunk and ran across the room, throwing herself into his arms. "Thank God you're safe!"

He pulled back from her enough to look into her face. He shook his head slightly. "No. Thank God *we're* safe."

Decimus explained what had happened and Chara sighed, leaning her forehead against his chest. His warm arms tightened gently around her, trying to impart some measure of consolation.

Chara gave a prayer of thanks to God for their safety. She felt comforted by the warmth of their embrace and her trembling slowed, then ceased altogether. Leaning back against Decimus' arm, she smiled into his face, suddenly realizing how dear he had become to her.

Decimus returned her smile, thankful himself for their safety. They had come so close to dying. What would have become of Chara if the attack had not been thwarted? As he continued to stare down into her eyes, the smile slowly slipped from his face. His gaze fastened on Chara's parted lips.

Chara could feel the pounding of Decimus' heart beneath her palms and her own began to race in response. Slowly he moved his face closer to hers until their lips were only a breath apart. Without knowing she had moved, Chara leaned closer, closing her eyes as their lips met.

As Chara melted into the embrace, she slid her hands up and around Decimus' neck. Warmth spread through her unlike any she had ever known. If only this moment would never cease.

Decimus suddenly broke the embrace as he heard thundering footsteps along the passageway. Galla slammed into the room.

"Are you all right?"

Chara nodded, her face suffusing with color. Galla grinned at her, unaware of the tension in the room.

"Well, at least one good thing came of this. Trophimus is no longer seasick."

Chara forced a laugh while Decimus smiled lamely. He was watching Chara intently, though Galla noticed nothing of their exchanged gazes.

"We shouldn't have any more problems with pirates. A Roman legion is patrolling the area. Apparently, they want these ships with supplies to Britannia to arrive intact."

"How long till we reach Massilia?" Decimus wanted to know.

"Soon. Another four days, perhaps less if the wind changes."

Decimus turned to Chara. "And when we reach Massilia, you will have your freedom."

six

Chara stared morosely at the approaching port of Massilia. Typical of ports anywhere, the docks were alive with activity. The hot sun's rays reflected against the tile roofs of the buildings.

Although the sun was warm against her skin, Chara felt cold inside. What would become of her now? Decimus promised her freedom upon reaching Massilia, because this far from Rome, Christians were in less danger.

Crazy man! What did he suppose she should do with her freedom? Find work somewhere? She let out her breath in frustration. Obviously, he wished to be free from her. Free from his *responsibility*.

Galla joined her at the rail. "Why such a pensive look on such a beautiful day?"

Chara smiled slightly. "What's to become of me, Galla? Where do I go from here? Trophimus, Caleb, and Thomas will have no problem finding work. They are strong and skilled, but what of me?"

Before he could answer, a soldier approached them, snapping a salute. "Centurion, the captain wishes to speak to you. He's below in the cargo hold."

Galla nodded, watching as the soldier turned and abruptly left them. He looked at Chara. "I'll talk to you later. Will you be all right?"

She smiled slightly. "I'll be fine. Go ahead."

The ship was sliding into the dock, the smoothness of it showing the sailors' expertise. Chara watched as the plank was dropped and men scrambled up in a surging horde.

Sacrarii carried their loads from wagons, waiting their turns at the scales. A stuppator balanced on scaffolding ready to caulk the ship that had just entered the dock. Chara marveled

68

at his ability to twist and turn, never losing his balance.

So intent was she on watching the scenes around her, Chara failed to hear Decimus come up behind her. She jumped when she heard his voice.

"I haven't seen you for a few days."

Chara glared at him. "'Twas not by *my* choice."

He had the grace to blush. True, he had avoided her for several days, ever since the attack on the ship. He hadn't known what to do or even what to think. His thoughts were even now in a turmoil about what to do with Chara.

"Chara, we need to talk."

Chara noticed the way Decimus refused to look her in the face. She felt her anger begin to rise. Well, he needn't bother worrying about her. She could take care of herself. He needn't worry that she would beg for his attention.

Galla was hurrying towards them, his lips set in a grim line. He pulled up beside Decimus. "Have you seen Thomas?"

Decimus frowned at the urgency of his tone. "Yes, he went below to see about our provisions."

"I'll go find him. You find Trophimus and Caleb and bring them to my quarters. Chara, you wait for us there. Hurry!"

Decimus didn't wait to ask questions. He hurried in the last direction he had seen the young Roman and the Jew. Chara watched them both disappear from sight and hastily went to the cabin to wait for them.

Galla was the first to arrive with Thomas, followed shortly by the others. Decimus closed the door behind them and they all looked to Galla for an explanation.

"We have a problem. The soldiers will be accompanying me all the way to Britannia."

Chara dropped to the bunk. Decimus' eyes grew wide. "They will be coming with *us*?"

Galla nodded. "There's more to it," he told them grimly, going over and sitting next to Chara. "It seems that I am not entirely free from suspicion after all, and that there is some question as to my *loyalties*. Captain Caltupa wasn't supposed to tell me this, but he has known me a long time."

"What does that mean for the rest of us?" Caleb wanted to know, his suspicions rising.

"It means," Galla told him tersely, "that you have to come with us."

Thomas surged away from the wall where he had been leaning. "To Britannia? Not if my life depended on it!"

Galla glared at him. "What about *six* lives?"

All in the room stared helplessly at Galla as the meaning of his words penetrated.

"Is there no other way?" Trophimus questioned.

"I have thought of a way for you to still have your freedom, but it will be risky." Galla waited until he was sure that his words had sunk in. "I will still give you your letters of manumission. I had them prepared before we left Rome. I will also give you part of the money that was given to us for this mission. As we travel overland, you are free to slip away."

"Just like that?" Caleb asked incredulously. "What happens if we're caught?"

Chara shivered at the look on Galla's face.

"Then we will all be on our way back to Rome, and most probably the arena."

Trophimus swallowed hard. "Then I'd suggest we not be caught."

Decimus frowned. "And what of Chara?"

Galla sucked in a breath, pressing his lips tightly together. "That is something I need to talk to you and Chara about alone. But before I do, are we all agreed so far?"

His look went from person to person, pausing lastly on Caleb. Slowly, the Jew nodded his head.

"Good. Then I need the three of you to go to the supply hold and help with the unloading."

Chara watched uneasily as the three others left the room. This was sounding more ominous by the minute. She swallowed apprehensively as Galla fixed his gaze upon her. He seemed hesitant to speak.

"Well?" Decimus prodded impatiently.

"I think the two of you need to marry." Galla dropped his bombshell and waited for a response. He hadn't long to wait.

"Are you out of your mind?" Decimus' fists clenched and unclenched at his sides.

Chara merely stared at Galla as though he had grown horns. His lips twitched. If the situation were not so serious, the looks on their faces would have been amusing.

"Before you take my head off, listen to me. The others will be leaving us soon. Eventually, they should be able to find passage to wherever they wish to go. That will leave the three of us. You, Decimus, will have your letter of manumission, as we agreed. But what of Chara?"

"I will do the same for her," Decimus told him impatiently. "I will hardly keep her as my slave. She will be free, just as the others will be."

"So, she will be a free woman alone in a foreign land. Or she can continue to accompany me, traveling with a group of soldiers. What then? What does that make her?"

Decimus felt his anger begin to rise. "Don't even suggest it."

"Would the two of you stop talking about me as though I weren't present? It's out of the question, anyway."

"Chara, it can be no other way. We have no choice," Galla remonstrated softly.

"I refuse," she told him adamantly.

"As do I."

Galla stared from one to the other. "Let me see if I can make it plainer. This is going to be a long, hard trip over a great distance. At times Chara will be the only woman within many miles. Now, if my men think her my slave, they may leave her alone for a time. But eventually this could cause difficulties. For her to sleep in my tent could cause. . .problems. They will think I should. . .share." He cleared his throat uncomfortably.

Chara stared at him uncomprehendingly, but Galla could see the dawning realization on Decimus' face.

"In any event," Galla continued, "she would have no privacy. I usually share my tents with my captains."

"Oh." Chara's tiny voice was the only sound for many minutes.

"I would marry you myself," Galla told her softly, "but Roman centurions are forbidden to marry."

Decimus and Chara exchanged looks briefly before they both quickly turned their eyes away.

"It's really the only way," Galla told them. "Unless, as I told Thomas, you want to risk six people's lives."

Chara dropped her head, her blond hair dropping down to conceal her face. "I can't."

Decimus raised his face to the ceiling, his teeth clenched.

Sighing, Galla turned to Decimus. "Let me talk to her alone for a minute, would you?"

Decimus glanced at Chara. Nodding his head briefly, he went to the door, turning back when Galla called him. "If Chara agrees, do you?"

Decimus looked briefly at Chara. He jerked his head in the affirmative and exited the room.

Before Galla could open his mouth, Chara attacked him with her words. "It will do you no good to *talk* to me, Galla. You could talk to me until the moon turned blue, and my answer would still be the same."

"Chara."

She leaped from the bunk, her hands curling at her sides. She turned to him. "No! I won't marry a man who doesn't love me."

Galla noticed she hadn't mentioned not loving Decimus. He was hopeful that he could win her to his way of thinking. And he didn't have much time.

"He does love you, only he doesn't know it yet."

Chara's eyes widened, her hands slowly uncurling at her sides. "I don't believe you," she whispered.

"I think you do. I don't know why you're fighting it. It's obvious to everyone that he cares for you."

"Oh, yes," she told him derisively. "He handles his responsibilities well. He takes care of me as well as he would a horse."

"Were you his responsibility on that auction block?"

Chara dropped back onto the bunk. "That was different. He felt pity for me." She glared into his eyes. "And if he allows this marriage it will be for the same reason."

Galla sighed. "What about you?"

"What about me?"

"Are you willing to let five men die and yourself as well? Do you think it's any easier for the others to play the part of slaves when they are so close to freedom?"

"That's different," she argued. "Their situation is temporary. Marriage is permanent."

"So is death." Galla didn't mean to be cruel or to make her feel guilty, but as a trained soldier he knew that sometimes one had to sacrifice oneself to save many. More was at stake here than their six lives.

Chara buried her head in her hands. "Oh, Galla! You're beginning to make sense, in an awful kind of way."

"Chara, listen to me. Decimus loves you, I can tell. You love him, that I can tell, also. So where would be the harm?"

Chara threw back her head, closing her eyes. "What if you're wrong?"

"I'm not. Trust me."

Was what Galla said possible? Could Decimus actually have some feelings for her? She gave a wry smile. "I once told Decimus that I would trust you with my life. It seems I have to make good my words."

Galla returned her smile, then reached out a hand and stroking a curled finger gently down her cheek. "You won't be sorry."

੨

Decimus stood beside Chara his face drawn and white. Chara stood as she usually did, her golden hair a veil that hid her true feelings. The priest of the temple of Zeus chanted words and watched as the two exchanged grain wafers. After chanting a few more words, he stepped to the side. Another priest used a pot of ink, registering their names on the prepared document with his stylus. Galla paid the priest, taking the rolled document from his hand, and the three of the them left the temple.

Married. The word echoed around and around in Chara's head. And by a pagan priest. All her life she had dreamed of what her wedding day would be like, and her dreams were nothing like the reality.

A tear trickled down her cheek. She prayed to God that this was not a horrible mistake. Looking at Decimus, she realized that he looked no happier than she. Did he really love her as Galla had suggested? She had wagered her whole life on one man's assurances. Her life and Decimus'.

Holding out her left hand, she stared at the ring that Decimus had purchased for her. A golden ring, the symbol of continuity, placed on the finger nearest her heart. She closed her eyes. One thing was certain, she loved Decimus. Now she had only to make sure that he loved her.

Decimus' voice broke the quiet that had shrouded them since they had left the temple. "Will there be any problem with the soldiers?"

Galla shook his head. "No. It's permitted for two slaves to marry as long as they have permission. Fortunately, you made their acceptance of the act easier because of the disturbance you made on the ship." He shrugged. "They will merely think I tired of her and gave her to you."

Decimus felt his face burn with anger. He had felt like killing the soldier with his bare hands for suggesting that he and Chara were doing something inappropriate. Now, the thought of the soldiers' assumption about Galla and Chara filled him with rage.

They walked slowly back to the inn where they had booked accommodations. Decimus thought of the document of manumission inside his pouch. It nestled safely next to the other document that declared him married. One scroll gave him his freedom, another took it away.

He sighed but refused to look at Chara. He had noticed the tear wending its way down her cheek, and his stomach had coiled tightly within him. He wanted to comfort her but didn't dare.

Opening the door to their room, Decimus allowed Chara to

precede him inside. He hesitated on the threshold.

Galla came up behind him. "I'm going to the baths," he told them, looking from one to the other.

Decimus seized on the opportunity. "I'll come with you."

Galla raised his eyebrows, but refrained from comment. Let the two of them work this out for themselves. He entered the room, going to his pack and taking out a clean tunic.

"Will you be all right by yourself?" he asked Chara quietly. She was looking at the floor, but she nodded her head slightly. He hesitated a moment before turning and leaving the room. Decimus followed closely on his heels.

Chara dropped on the bed and began to cry, deep, wracking sobs. So much had happened to her since her mother had died, and now here she was in a strange city on her wedding day, alone.

Thoughts whirled around in her head, giving her no peace. Where did she go from here? What was to become of her now? The words of Jesus came to her mind. *Come to Me, all you who are weary and burdened, and I will give you rest.* Closing her eyes, she did just that. Slowly, her prayers brought the peace she was seeking. No matter what happened, God was with her. Exhausted, she slept.

❧

Galla sat cross-legged on the pool floor, scraping his skin with the strigil and shaking the water off onto the mosaic tiles. Decimus sat beside him, his strong legs dangling in the cool water. He knew that Galla had something he wanted to say, but for some reason he was keeping his silence.

"You may as well say it," Decimus told him at last.

Galla looked at him innocently. "Say what?"

"Whatever it is that is causing you to turn blue from choking it back," Decimus told him, aggravated.

Laughing, Galla continued to scrape his skin. "If I'm turning blue, it's from the water in the frigidarium."

"I think not," Decimus disagreed softly.

Galla regarded Decimus with veiled eyes. The Briton had changed much over the last few weeks. He had a maturity about him now that rested easily upon his shoulders. He was no longer the boy Galla had originally thought him.

"Do you love Chara?" Galla finally asked. He watched Decimus' brows instantly draw down in a frown.

"Why are you asking?"

"She's a special lady. I don't want to see her hurt."

Decimus glared at Galla, but the older man was unaffected. A few angry looks wouldn't frighten him, especially when he wanted to make sure someone he cared about would not be hurt.

"It's no concern of yours," Decimus finally told him.

"I disagree. I happen to love Chara, too. I want to see her happy."

The sparkle in Decimus' eyes intensified. "What do you mean you love her?"

"You know what I mean, so don't pretend you don't. She's like a sister to me. If not for you, I might have tried to make it otherwise, but I knew with you around, I stood no chance. She loves you."

Decimus sighed, lying back against the marble tiles. He closed his eyes as though that would ward off any other thoughts. "I know."

The admission surprised Galla. "You *know* she loves you? Then where's the problem?"

Decimus lifted his legs from the water and got quickly to his feet. "The problem lies within me. I'm not sure I love her. Not that way. I care for her, yes, but. . ."

"There's someone else?"

Decimus sighed. "There was. I thought I loved her, too, but the feelings. . .I don't know anymore."

"I see." Galla studied him a moment, then rose to his feet to stand beside him. He wasn't sure just what to say. How could he reassure Decimus that what he felt was real when in actuality Galla didn't know? Only Decimus knew what was in his own mind.

They walked to the changing rooms, retrieving their tunics from the shelves and donning them. Decimus followed Galla into the street. Although his body felt rejuvenated, his mind was still in a shambles.

The sun was setting as they threaded their way through the streets to the inn. Decimus felt guilty when he realized that Chara might have wished to go to the baths, too. Instead, she had deferred to his wish to be away from her.

When they reached the room, Galla began to gather his things together. Decimus watched him, alarmed. "What are you doing?"

Raising his brows, Galla continued what he was doing. "I'm clearing out. I'll stay with the troops."

Chara came to her feet, twisting her hands together in front of her. "That's not necessary."

"I think it is."

Decimus and Chara exchanged glances. Decimus felt the heat rise to his own face as he watched the color flow into Chara's. He turned to Galla. "It's really not necessary for you to leave. I mean, on the trip north there will be little privacy."

"Exactly," Galla agreed. "You need some time alone *now*." He went to the door and opened it. Giving one last look at the couple, he left.

Chara and Decimus stood facing each other, eyes going everywhere but toward each other.

"Are you hungry?" Decimus wanted to know.

Chara shook her head. "Not really."

"Well, I am. How about if we go downstairs and get a meal?"

Chara shrugged. "If you want to."

Anything to prolong the time when they would retire, Decimus decided. He followed Chara down the stairs into the main room below. Already a crowd was beginning to congregate. Feeling eyes upon them, Decimus decided that maybe this had not been a good idea after all.

The proprietor showed them to a table set back in a corner, and Decimus breathed a sigh of relief. A few moments later the man returned with a flask of wine and a platter of meats and fruits.

Chara picked up a piece of cheese and began to nibble.

Slowly her appetite returned to her. She had not eaten since the meal at breakfast, of which she had consumed little.

Decimus poured himself a drink and one for Chara. The liquid slid coolly down his dry throat. He watched as Chara sipped at her own drink. Everything she did spoke of daintiness and refinement. Where had she learned such things?

"Tell me about your family."

Surprised, Chara looked up. "What do you wish to know?"

"You told me of your mother in Galilee, but what happened to her later? How did she get to Gaul?"

Chara smiled, her eyes taking on a faraway look. "The family who owned her treated her as a daughter, not as a slave. She was free to go anywhere she chose. My father was a merchant on his way back to Gaul from Syria when he saw my mother at the watering well. When he saw her, he fell in love with her. The family she was with gave her her freedom, and their blessings. They were sad to see her go, but joyful that she had found such happiness. I was twelve when my father died."

She paused, her brow furrowing in a frown. "She was a wonderful mother and she taught me everything she could about being a lady. When my father died, something died within her. She was never the same." She stopped, picking the meat from the chicken leg she was holding. "My stepfather married her a year later. She was a beautiful woman, and many men wanted her, but she chose him. Probably, I think, because he was wealthy and she thought he would look after us." Chara's voice softened. "I think he drank so much because he knew my mother didn't love him. He never said anything, but he knew all the same."

Decimus regretted asking, especially since he knew how the story ended.

The room was becoming more crowded. Crude language filtered the spaces around them, making Decimus wince. Color flooded Chara's cheeks as she heard some of the ribald jokes and coarse laughter.

"Are you finished with your meal?"

Chara nodded, rising to her feet. They made their way

toward the stairs. Decimus gritted his teeth as he noticed the men in the room look their way. He heard their sly laughter, and he felt like shouting to the whole crazy place that they were legally married.

When they reached the room, Chara breathed a sigh of relief. If she had had to remain downstairs one moment longer, she thought she would have screamed.

Decimus stood leaning with his back against the door, watching Chara drift about the room. She picked up a garment, folding it and laying it across the room's only chair. Decimus' eyes flicked to the bed and he swallowed hard.

Going over, he began to pull blankets from the bed. Chara stared at him in surprise. He went back to the door, laying the coverings on the floor. When Chara continued to stare at him, he shrugged his shoulders. "I thought it might be safer for me to sleep here. You can have the bed. That way if anyone tries to enter, I will know about it." The excuse sounded lame even to his own ears.

Chara was relieved, but piqued at the same time. Would she ever understand this man? Sighing, she began to prepare herself for bed. She could feel Decimus' eyes on her as she began to comb out her hair with her fingers. Deciding that she could go to the baths in the morning when few others would be around, she lay down in her clothes. Within moments she was fast asleep.

Decimus watched as Chara's breathing became even. Finally, his own breathing slowed its erratic pace. He shook his head slightly. Getting up, he crossed to where Chara lay sleeping. He watched her for a long time, awed that she belonged to him. Not as a slave, but as a wife. Fear like none he had ever known before filled his entire being. He didn't know *how* to be a husband. He wasn't sure he wanted to know.

He went back and lay down on his cold pallet. Lifting his eyes to the ceiling, he began to pray. *Lord, help me to know what to do. Help me to do what's right.* Glancing again at Chara's sleeping form he added, *Lord, help me to love this woman.*

seven

Decimus lifted Chara to the back of the huge roan gelding. Climbing up behind her, he settled himself firmly in the saddle, wrapping one arm securely around her waist. Memories of riding with Diana in the hills around Ephesus floated through his mind. His job had been to protect her and see that she came to no harm. He felt the same responsibility now.

Instead of traversing the distance through Gaul to the Loire River by foot, Galla had decided to mount the troops. Since the journey could be covered more swiftly by mount, he felt the expense was justified, and there would be the added benefit of using the horses later, if necessary, for battle.

Galla glanced swiftly about him, checking to see that all were accounted for. Thomas, Trophimus, and Caleb, each driving a wagon full of trade goods, gave him a quick nod of acknowledgement.

Captain Caltupa approached from the front of the column. "We're ready, centurion."

Looking around once more, Galla nodded his head and mounted his own horse. "Let's go," he told them, moving forward to the front of the entourage. Decimus and Chara would follow at the rear with the wagons, along with several of the soldiers.

As they moved forward through the city, the sun was suddenly hidden behind clouds that were steadily thickening in the sky. A mist of rain began to fall, causing Chara to shiver. Decimus felt her body begin to tremble.

"Are you cold?"

Although the weather was still somewhat warm, the wetness cooled the temperatures considerably, a precursor of the winter to come.

Chara shook her head. "No." She looked quickly about her at the countryside of her birth and shivered again. "I just hope the weather is not an omen of things to come."

Decimus was surprised at her morbid turn of thoughts. Noticing the direction of her gaze, he thought he understood. "You needn't be afraid of your stepbrother. He has no control over your life now."

They picked their way along the cobbled road as the rain increased in tempo. Before long they were soaked. Decimus tried to shield Chara as much as possible, but the moisture crept everywhere, filling every available space.

When Chara spoke, her voice seemed to come from a long distance. Decimus realized that she was speaking more to herself than to him.

"I never thought I would see my homeland again," she told him softly. "And now, here I am, back where I started from. I used to think that Franco was the closest thing to Satan that a person could be, but that was before I knew about Nero. I now realize that with Franco, it was just jealousy. I don't think he meant me any *real* harm."

Decimus shifted slightly in the saddle, refraining from comment. Surely her stepbrother knew what atrocities were perpetrated upon slaves, especially female ones.

"I can forgive him more easily now," Chara told him. "For if not for him, I never would have met you."

Decimus swallowed hard. There it was again, that complete trust in him. That faith that he was what was meant for her life. Her belief in him made him want to stand a little straighter, be a little stronger. He wanted to live up to her ideals, but he was afraid that he couldn't.

Before long they reached a thick copse of woods. The road continued through it, winding its way among the thick shrubs and trees. The rain fell softer here, and the column suddenly came to a stop.

A young soldier came riding toward them. "Centurion Galla says we are to stop here for a short spell. If you have any needs to attend to, do it quickly."

Decimus quickly dismounted, tying the reins to a small tree. Reaching up, he lifted Chara from the saddle and lowered her to the ground.

"I have a leather cloak in my pack that will help keep the rain off you," he told her, digging to find the article he was looking for. "You need to change out of that wet tunic."

Nodding, Chara rummaged around until she found a suitable change of clothes. Clutching the tunic to her chest, she looked hesitantly around her. Seeing her predicament, Decimus rolled the cloak into a ball, tucking it under his own tunic. He took Chara by the hand and led her a short distance into the woods until he found a large tree that shielded her from the others.

"Change quickly," he told her, "or someone might come looking for us."

While Chara was changing behind the tree, Decimus availed himself of the opportunity to quickly change his own garments. He pulled the leather cloak he had purchased for himself around him, thankful for the fur lining. The temperatures were dropping rapidly, and he was beginning to wonder if winter was going to come early to this part of the world. He certainly hoped not, because they still had a long way to travel.

Chara emerged from the trees, her bright blue tunic making her look for all the world like a small bird amongst the huge forest. Decimus handed her her own cloak and waited impassively while she secured it around her shoulders.

"Better?" he asked.

She smiled then, and Decimus felt his heart give a leap.

"Much."

They quickly made their way back to the others, who were already mounting up. Decimus once again lifted Chara to the saddle and positioned himself behind her. He had purchased Chara her own mount, but for now it was being used to carry supplies. Decimus smiled slightly. No matter. He was rather enjoying the arrangement.

The road continued through the forest for many miles.

Decimus had never seen so many trees in his life, and although they provided protection from the elements, they also made him leery. Shadows seemed to move through the interior of the trees, and Decimus thought he saw once a pair of glowing yellow eyes.

Before long the road widened out and the trees began to thin, ending as abruptly as they had begun. The road led down into a green valley, and although the rain hit them with greater force, Decimus was glad to be free from the forest.

Dusk was falling when Galla called a halt for the night. Everyone began to quickly ready their shelters. Chara tried to help Decimus and Caleb, but she was more in the way than anything else. Shrugging, she abandoned the effort, going instead to sit on a rock near a stream of water.

Trophimus was already there watering the horses. He smiled when she reached him.

"I have muscles that ache that I didn't even know I had."

Chara smiled in sympathy. "I can agree with that, although I think perhaps a wagon seat might be a little more comfortable than a horse."

Decimus found them arguing good-naturedly with each other about the advantages of traveling on horseback versus in a wagon seat. One eyebrow cocked upward and he smiled.

"What, Trophimus, you think yourself ill used?"

Trophimus grinned back at him unabashedly. "I would gladly trade places with you."

Decimus' smile dimmed somewhat. "Perhaps. But I am not inclined to grant you that opportunity." He turned to Chara. "Do you think you can fix us a meal? Thomas will help you."

"Of course," she told him testily. She was aggravated that he continued to see her as little more than a child. What did he think, that she was useless? He might be surprised at what she could do.

Two pairs of male eyes followed her progress, the angry sway of her hips speaking to them more clearly than any words. Decimus turned to find Trophimus hiding a grin. He cocked an eyebrow at the young Roman, shrugging his shoulders. "What did I say?"

Trophimus turned quickly away, picking up a water bag and hefting it over his shoulder. "Don't ask me. She's *your* wife."

Decimus sat down on the rock Chara had so recently vacated. Women were so unpredictable.

Galla joined him, arching an eyebrow in inquiry. "Something bothering you?"

Reaching down, Decimus picked up a stick and began to draw circles in the sand. Water dripped down his nose and puddled at his feet.

"You're going to catch your death out here," Galla told him impatiently. "Come back to camp and get into some dry things."

Only then did Decimus realize that he had left his fur-lined cloak in the tent Caleb and he had erected for their group. Lifting his head, he stared hard into Galla's curious eyes. "I didn't sleep in the same bed with her last night."

Something flickered in Galla's own dark gaze before he pressed his lips tightly together. "Well, I'm afraid you had better here. If you leave an opening for these soldiers, you'll have to accept the consequences." He stopped, letting his words sink in. "She's your *wife*. I'd suggest you treat her like one so that she is afforded the respect she deserves."

Decimus rose to his feet, angry that Galla should so chastise him. Slowly the anger faded and he realized that Galla only meant the best for both Chara and himself. Galla slapped him on the back.

"Come on. I'm hungry."

They walked back to camp in silence, although it was a congenial one. There would be much they would go through together in the future, Decimus realized, and they would have no one but each other to depend on.

Chara watched Decimus and Galla coming and rose to prepare them a plate. Soldiers traveling long distances depended on dried fruits and nuts, and that was what they ate for the most part. However, one young soldier had availed himself of the opportunity to practice his bow shooting and had brought down a young stag in the forest. The meat had been distributed around and the soldier was strutting around the fire as he received congratulations from the others. Chara couldn't help but smile at the young lad's cockiness.

Decimus took a seat beside Chara, while Galla sat across from them. Lines of fatigue were etched around his mouth and Chara decided that there was something troubling his mind.

"What is bothering you, Galla?" she asked him softly.

He looked at her a moment before his lips finally turned up in a smile. "Nothing that you can help me with," he told her finally. "Just soldier things."

She would have asked him more, but Caleb rose to his feet. "I don't know about the rest of you, but I'm for bed."

Thomas rose also. "I'm all for that. How about you, Trophimus?"

Trophimus lifted his plate for their inspection. "I'm more hungry than tired. I have to finish eating first."

Chara leaned her hands towards the fire, trying to get as close as possible. The rain had stopped at last, but with darkness, the cold intensified, tiny crystals of ice forming on every wet surface. Even in her fur-lined cloak she was chilled.

Galla left to join his men, and Decimus and Trophimus continued to talk. Their soft murmuring voices soon lulled Chara into a state of semiwakefulness and her head began nodding forward. She didn't realize the voices around her had stopped until she felt herself lifted into strong arms. She heard Trophimus's voice as though in a dream.

"She must be exhausted."

Chara felt herself carried into the tent and laid gently on a mat. She felt bereft when Decimus' warm arms left her. A moment later she felt a fur blanket draped over her. Shivering, she pulled it close against her, huddling into a ball. Before long her deep breathing told Decimus she was sound asleep.

He watched her several minutes, a soft smile curving his lips. She reminded him of a child, her lashes feathered against her smooth cheeks. The smile slowly faded. She hadn't *felt* like a child in his arms. She had felt warm, and a shiver of yearning ran through him.

Shaking his head, he left the tent to rejoin Trophimus. They talked a long time about many things. Until that moment, Decimus hadn't really seen the young Roman as anything other than part of their entourage. Watching the boy, Decimus realized how homesick he must be. No matter how decadent Rome had been, it was still his home, the only one he had ever known.

Trophimus finally rose to his feet, stretching his arms above his head. "Well, I hate to leave you out here all alone, but I'm tired. I'll see you in the morning."

Decimus watched as the tent swallowed him. He turned his eyes back to the fire, continuing to gaze at it for a long time. Galla's words kept echoing through his mind. Rising slowly to his feet, he made his way toward the tent.

He crossed to where Chara lay curled asleep. Lifting the cover gently, he crawled in beside her. He lay tense, his hands behind his head, listening to the sound of her breathing. Suddenly, she rolled over, throwing one arm across his chest and her knee across his legs. His breathing almost stopped.

Several minutes he lay tensely waiting for her to move. Realizing she wasn't going to, he exhaled slowly. Carefully, he moved one arm around her, pulling her tighter against him. She smiled in her sleep, cuddling closer. Decimus gritted his teeth. He began to count in his head. Finally, his body began to relax and exhaustion took over, his eyes closing in sleep.

≈

When Chara awoke in the morning, she found the tent empty. Noises from outside indicated that the others were preparing to leave. Rising quickly to her feet, she stumbled outside.

Decimus was strapping a pack on one of the horses. He glanced quickly at her, then away. "You better hurry and get something to eat. Galla wants to leave within the hour."

"Why didn't you wake me?" she asked, hurrying to his

behind. He smiled slightly seeing the contented smile on Chara's face as she leaned back against her husband. Decimus, on the other hand, was not smiling at all. Galla frowned, wondering what was going through his mind.

Galla would have been surprised if he could have read Decimus' thoughts. He was beginning to like this being married bit. The one thing that bothered him was the fact that the farther they moved north, the closer he was taking Chara into danger. He had no idea what to expect when they reached Britannia. It had been years since he had been there, and his memories were foggy. He had no definite livelihood there, no security to offer her.

He could dimly remember a midsummer's night, a huge fire, and priests dressed in robes. Why was it that thought stood out so clearly in his mind? When he tried to remember more, his thoughts shied away and his mind went blank.

The sun rose higher in the sky, its rays warming the air around them until they began to perspire. The extremes in temperature were uncomfortable, and he wondered if they were typical of Gaul.

Unlike yesterday, no forest offered them shade today from the intense rays of the sun. Just when Decimus thought he could stand the heat no longer, a gentle breeze sprung up, blowing against his face. Chara leaned into it, closing her eyes with a smile.

A sudden disturbance behind them caused Decimus to swing around. He could hear angry voices and cursing, and the caravan came to a sudden halt.

Galla quickly made his way to the rear. "What's going on here?"

One of the soldiers that had been traveling rearguard came forward. "It's the wagons, centurion. Two of them have broken an axle."

Galla quickly dismounted, making his way past the guards who were standing around complaining of the heat. As he passed, they snapped to attention.

Caleb stood beside his wagon, scratching his head. Thomas leaned against the other wagon, shrugging his shoulders when Galla approached. Each wagon was loaded to the maximum. It would take hours to unload and fix them.

Decimus came up behind Galla. "What are you going to do?"

Galla caught a glimmer in Caleb's eyes before Caleb turned away to study the broken axle. Without taking his eyes from the Jew, Galla answered Decimus. "The last mile marker showed us to be about four miles from the statio." He paused, taking note that the sun was sinking rapidly.

The captain made his way to Galla's side, snapping a salute. "What do you wish us to do, centurion?"

Galla sighed. "Take the troops to the garrison." He turned to Decimus. "You take Chara and go with them. There will be an inn to stay at. I'll stay with the wagons, along with my slaves and a couple of the soldiers. We should be fine until morning." Turning back to the captain, he told him, "First thing in the morning, bring replacement wagons. Have the smith come with you and he can repair these wagons and return them to the garrison."

Caltupa looked uncomfortable. "Centurion, would it not be better for me to remain with the wagons?"

"These supplies are my responsibility, captain. You have your orders."

Galla and Decimus exchanged glances before Galla quickly turned away, giving orders for the unloading of the wagons.

Decimus went back to where Chara was waiting patiently on their horse. "What's wrong?" she asked.

"Two of the wagons have broken down. They'll have to remain here until tomorrow. We're going on with the other wagons and the rest of the troops."

He climbed up behind her, taking the reins from her hand.

"What of Galla and the others?" she wanted to know.

Decimus looked over her head, clicking his tongue at the horse. Slowly they moved forward. "They're staying with the wagons until tomorrow."

Chara frowned, glancing behind her. Something didn't seem quite right, but she couldn't decide what it was. Looking up at Decimus, she found his expression closed and unreadable.

The captain picked up the pace in order to reach the garrison before nightfall. The last rays of the sun were setting behind the hills when they pulled to a stop in the courtyard of an inn.

"I'll leave you here," the captain informed him. "But don't try to run away. I'll leave word with the proprietor to keep an eye on you. Do you understand?"

Decimus understood all too well. And although he was not particularly fond of inns, he would welcome a respite from the soldiers' company.

He lifted Chara down from the horse, and she leaned against him until her legs strengthened beneath her. Dark circles around her eyes spoke of her fatigue.

Taking her by the hand, he led her to a table in the corner of the inn. Glancing around, he noticed very few customers, and those were mainly soldiers who had wanted a change from the garrison. Their interest quickened when they noticed Chara, and Decimus was reluctant to leave her, but he had to stable the horse.

"I'll be right back," he told her. "When the proprietor comes, order us something to eat."

Although many eyes followed her movements, the soldiers kept a respectful distance. Decimus returned, hurrying them through their meal. This time when they retired to their room, they did not quibble over who would sleep where. When Chara closed her eyes that night, she was snuggled safely in her husband's arms.

eight

Decimus watched Chara ambling along in front of the wagon he was driving. She rode a horse well. He caught the eye of Caltupa and almost smiled at the man's menacing glower. After all, he had reason to scowl. During the night Thomas and Caleb had disappeared, slipped away when no one was looking. Decimus grinned. Even Galla had been unaware of their disappearance until morning.

Captain Caltupa had wanted to organize a search immediately, but Galla had forestalled him, telling him that getting the supplies and men to Britannia was more important than the disappearance of two slaves.

Decimus had been surprised when Trophimus had driven his wagon into the compound behind the others. He hadn't had time to talk to the young Roman, but he was curious as to his reasons for staying. Had he not been able to slip away with the others? Surely Caleb would have waited for him, though everyone knew that the Jew had no love for Romans.

Chara turned and caught his eye and her smile lit up her face. How was it that he had considered her rather plain in the beginning? She had beauty much like that of young Sara, the kind of beauty that seemed to come from within. Hadn't the Apostle Peter said something to that effect?

Decimus felt butterflies tumbling about inside him. How long could he continue to sleep with his wife and do nothing besides hold her gently? Every time he held her close, he felt himself drawn perilously near to holding her tighter, pressing his lips to hers, and. . .He frowned, considering the consequences.

If Chara were to become pregnant. . .the thought terrified

him. He had no idea what would happen over the next several months, and he wasn't about to take such a risk. Very possibly not one of them would come out of this alive. He could remember little of his life as a boy, but the stories circulating around the empire did nothing to calm his fears. Did the Druids truly offer human sacrifices to their gods? What kind of reception would they give to someone trying to teach them of another God, one who didn't desire sacrifices at all?

But was that really true? Didn't the Lord want His people to give their whole lives to Him? Even to the point of facing lions in an arena of Rome? There was no greater sacrifice than the one Antipus and Agrippina had made.

They traveled without incident the remainder of the day. The sun spilled its rays warmly across the verdant hillsides. Rolling, undulating hills met the eye wherever one turned. The scent of pine from the forests in the distance drifted to them on the cooling breeze.

Decimus noted that they were passing another mile marker. Every ten miles or so, one could find another statio where soldiers could refresh their horses or stay for the night. According to his calculations, this made the ninth marker. He sighed, wondering if Galla would choose to press on. Since they had only come nine miles, he decided that Galla would most likely choose to continue.

They passed one small village and then another. Everywhere they went, they were greeted with hostility. Fear and hatred emanated from the eyes of the people they passed.

Galla called a halt when the sun was high in the sky, for they had reached a small stream and needed the time to water the horses. Decimus helped Chara to the ground, keeping one arm protectively around her as his eyes skimmed the nearby forest. Deciding that nothing was in the vicinity, he walked with her into the woods. Keeping his back to her, he watched the others mingling about.

When Chara rejoined Decimus, he was sitting on a boulder next to the stream, allowing the cool water to run over his bare feet. He smiled up at her, taking her hand and pulling her down beside him.

"Try it," he told her. "It's refreshing."

Feeling like a child again, she slid her sandals from her feet and plunged them into the cold water. Squealing, she pulled them quickly back.

"It's like ice!"

Decimus grinned. "That's because it comes from the mountains."

Glancing up, Decimus noticed that Caltupa wasn't far away. The man's constant vigil was beginning to wear on Decimus' not-so-good humor.

Noticing the direction of her husband's fierce gaze, Chara turned her head. She turned back to the spring, cupping her hands and letting the water run through her fingers.

"Did you know that Caleb and Thomas were going to leave last night?" she whispered.

Decimus focused his attention on his wife, trying to forget the other man's presence. "I thought they might. It was no accident that *both* their axles broke."

"I wondered." Her eyes met his. "But why didn't Trophimus go with them?"

Decimus shrugged. "I haven't talked to him yet. I don't know."

A shadow blocked out the sun. "Time to leave."

Rising slowly to his feet, Decimus gave the man glare for glare, his muscles rippling as he clenched his fists at his side. Chara moved quickly to place herself between them, taking Decimus by the hand.

"We were just coming, captain."

Decimus was aggravated that the man followed so closely behind. Grinning wryly, he realized that it hadn't taken him long to appreciate his freedom. How long he would have to suffer the company of the soldiers, he didn't know, but one thing was for sure, he hoped he never knew the bonds of slavery again.

Decimus lifted Chara back on her horse, helping her adjust herself to the saddle. Laying a hand against the mare's shoulder, he smiled up at Chara. "You ride a horse well."

She smiled. "My father taught me when I was a child. I have missed it."

"What other skills have you that I know nothing about?"

Chara arched a supercilious brow. "Only time will tell."

For some unknown reason this only served to make Decimus uncomfortable. The smile fled from his face, and turning, he made his way back to his wagon, climbing aboard. Chara had already started to move forward when he clicked to his horses to begin the journey.

When they reached the statio that evening, Galla chose to remain at the inn instead of the garrison.

"If I don't, I have no doubt that Caltupa will. He seems obsessed with making sure no other slaves escape." Galla grinned wryly as he loosened his saddle. "He already doubts my expertise in handling the matter."

The captain was obviously reluctant to leave and return to the garrison. Only direct orders had made him submit.

"He seems to have developed a personal vendetta against me," Decimus told Galla quietly, hoping that Chara wouldn't hear.

"I noticed." Galla studied the man beside him, but could see no evidence of fear. "I wouldn't let it worry you. As long as you're considered my property there's not much he can do about it."

Chara was waiting for them, a platter of meats, fruits, vegetables, and cheeses on the table in front of her. A serving girl brought them drinks and then left them alone.

"Back to the beginning," Galla told them, shaking his head. "It seems we are fated to spend our nights together."

Decimus realized what he was trying to say. If Galla didn't remain with them, Caltupa most assuredly would. He shrugged. "No problem. As you said, we have done so before."

Galla picked up a knife and began drawing circles on the

wooden platter. "By tomorrow we should reach the Loire River. We'll take the river west to the Narrow Sea that separates Britannia from Gaul."

"More travel by sea?" Chara questioned, less than enthusiastically.

Galla nodded. "It should take us only a few weeks all together."

A group of soldiers noisily seated themselves at the table next to them. They noticed Galla and quickly rose to their feet, snapping a salute.

"Centurion! We didn't see you."

Decimus had no doubt that was because their eyes had been on Chara. She flushed, the color making her lovelier.

Galla nodded his head and the soldiers resumed their seats. Although the men were talking among themselves, the wine they continued to consume loosened their tongues considerably. Their strident voices could be heard clearly around the room.

"I hear we're going to mount another counterattack in Britannia," one soldier slurred. "I'd have thought we would have taught them a lesson seven years back when we slaughtered Queen Boudicca's forces." He gave a course laugh. "No matter. I won't mind another chance at wiping out the likes of them Druids."

Galla noticed heads turned their way. Many in the room were not soldiers, but civilians from nearby towns and provinces. As far as he knew, the counterattack in Britannia was still a secret. More than likely the drunken soldier was guessing, but his mouth could very well cost lives.

Galla rose quickly to his feet, striding to the table beside him. "On your feet, soldier."

The man stared up at him in confusion, his stupefied expression giving him a comical appearance. Slowly, recognition dawned and he struggled to his feet. Swaying, he snapped a salute that landed somewhere near his right arm.

Another soldier, less drunk, rose from his seat. Galla glared at him angrily. "Take your comrade back to the garrison. Now!" He glanced around at the others. "All of you! Back to the garrison."

Grumbling, they got to their feet and started for the door. Galla returned to his seat, his eyes still on the door.

Decimus studied the Roman and began to have serious misgivings. How much of Galla's heart was truly Roman, and exactly how much could he be counted on? Decimus decided he would have to watch more closely in the future.

❧

The town of Lugdunum was much like any other town they had passed thus far, only larger. Here were more of the civilizing influences of the empire. Since it was the largest town near the Loire River, there was much trade and commerce here. The streets were thronged with people going about their daily business.

Galla smiled in appreciation when he noticed that this city boasted a public bath. "I know where I intend to spend the evening," he told them cheerily.

Decimus smiled. "I could stand to use the facilities myself." He turned to Chara. "How about you?"

Chara readily agreed. Tomorrow would find them on board ship again, and it would likely be days before they saw land. They all agreed that food could wait, so after renting a room at an inn, they headed for the baths.

Unlike most of the public baths in Rome and Ephesus, these baths had separate facilities for men and women. Chara sighed with relief. The Romans would no doubt think these people too provincial, but Chara appreciated their modesty.

Feeling refreshed, they sat down to a hot meal at the inn. Chara felt her stomach rumble, her nose twitching at the smell of the roasted chicken placed before them. She dipped her bread in a bowl of gravy, licking her fingers as she consumed the delicious food.

The noise in the inn was growing as the evening progressed. Remembering past nights, Decimus knew there would be little sleep for him. He was always amazed that Chara could sleep so peacefully with the noise all around. The ruckus would finally abate sometime after midnight when the inn was closed for the night.

They made their way to their room, Galla holding the small oil lamp used to light the passage. Decimus followed him into the room, carrying their fur rugs. Experience had taught them that tiny uninvited guests usually resided in the bedding provided by the inns.

Chara seated herself on the only chair available, smiling slightly as her fingers traced the graffiti etched on the walls. *Arestes loves Portia*, read one. Did Portia love poor Arestes, Chara wondered, or had Arestes merely dreamed of his loved one? Were they married? Some of the scratched messages left Chara blushing. She decided to refrain from reading any others.

Decimus had positioned their bed as far from the door as possible, but Chara noticed that Galla placed his pallet directly in front of the portal. She wondered if they were expecting any trouble.

Even though the din from below penetrated through the floor, Chara was asleep almost as soon as her head found its position on Decimus' shoulder. He pulled her closer, smiling down at her innocent features.

As quiet descended for the night, Decimus found himself able to think. The woman he held so securely in his arms was a part of his life now, no matter what happened. His heart was hopelessly entwined with hers. As he did every night, he prayed for their safety. Was he jumping from the coals into the fire? Only God knew, and He wasn't telling.

❧

Chara watched the sailors and the captain preparing their sacrifice before the ship was about to sail. She shuddered at the cries of the lamb as it struggled ineffectively against it's captors. She turned and fled to the other end of the ship.

Stevedores carried amphoras of wine and olive oil in a never ending procession below decks. Grain would be poured directly into the hold and the amphoras' pointed ends shoved deeply into the grain. The amphoras would be stacked in tiers as high as the hold itself.

Chara marveled at the size of the ship they would be sailing on. One hundred-eighty feet from end to end. Enough space for all the supplies they had brought from Rome plus the trade goods from Gaul to Britannia. For this trip, she and Decimus would be sleeping on deck, as would Galla. All available space was being used to store the goods to Britannia.

Trophimus joined her at the rails, his eyes sparkling merrily. One thing could be said for Trophimus, he enjoyed life. Smiling, she leaned back against the rails. "Why didn't you go with the others?"

He wrinkled his nose watching the sky above. Finally, he shrugged his shoulders. "I'm not sure. Something told me to stay with you and Decimus." His look was penetrating. "Does that make sense to you?"

A dark cloud of foreboding momentarily darkened her happiness. She lay a hand on his arm. "Trophimus, you could be free to do anything you please, yet you remained with us. I don't know what voice made you do what you did, but I know I'm glad. I would miss you."

He smiled into her soft brown eyes, a mirror image of his own.

Chara returned his smile, realizing that he was a very handsome boy. She wondered what the future held in store for him. She had noticed women look his way at every town they passed. He would have no hard time finding himself a wife. She felt a decidedly motherly instinct where he was concerned.

Decimus and Galla joined them.

"Are we going to sail soon?" Chara asked them.

Galla smiled wryly. "It took a few more denarii than I expected, but it looks like we'll be heading out soon. We need to be our way quickly so that we are not still as sea when the first storms of winter set in." He turned toward the deck. "We had better find ourselves a spot, before all the good spots are taken."

Sailors scurried to carry out their business. Chara watched them with interest. Each time she had sailed, she had been impressed with the sailors and their expertise. They scrambled about the ship like busy little ants.

At last the huge ship's sails filled with wind. The boat creaked and swayed, tossed gently by the river. Chara stood with Decimus at the rail, watching the lights of the port city fade into the distance. The sun was setting in an awesome display of radiant reds and oranges.

"Red sky at night, sailors' delight," Decimus told her, putting an arm around her shoulder. Chara snuggled into his embrace, as much for the need to be close to him as the need for warmth.

Darkness descended and the stars appeared in all their brilliance. The inky black sky seemed alive with the glow of a million shimmering lights. The moon rose round and orange above the horizon.

They stood a long time marveling at God's universe. How could a person witness such sights and be immune to the Almighty's presence? Surely sailors should be closer to God than anyone, if they would only listen for His voice.

Watching Decimus' face in the moonlight, Chara wondered what he was thinking. Was he thinking about their unusual marriage? Was he regretting it? She considered asking, but she was afraid she wouldn't like the answer.

She knew he desired her. She could tell from his reactions when he held her in his arms, but he never made any move to make their relationship into a real marriage.

"What are you thinking?" she ventured.

His eyes flickered briefly before he looked down. "I was just wondering what I will find at the end of this journey." He leaned his forearms against the rails and stared pensively out at the dark waters. Chara felt chilled when he moved away. "Will I find any of my family? I fear my parents are both dead, though I do not know for certain. But is my sister still alive? Would I know her if I saw her? I don't even know where to begin."

"You could begin by praying. Asking for God's guidance."

"I have."

"Then trust Him to show you the way. He'll never forsake you."

Decimus smiled, lifting one blond brow. The breeze blew a lock of hair across his forehead, and Chara was tempted to reach up and push it back for him. What would he think of such a loving gesture?

"I'm beginning to realize that more and more. Every time I think some catastrophe has just about ruined my life, it turns into a blessing."

Chara smiled softly in return. "I have found the same to be true."

Decimus pushed away from the rails, taking Chara by the hand. "Come. It's time to retire for the night, before our spot is taken away."

They settled themselves on the furs beside Galla and Trophimus. Caltupa had relaxed his guard, obviously no longer concerned with the slaves' escape.

Galla was describing Britannia to Trophimus. Although he had never seen his homeland, he knew it well from his father's descriptions. One of the younger soldiers was listening closely to everything he said. Leaning up on one elbow, he fixed Galla with a fearful gaze.

"I hear they offer human sacrifices to their gods," he told them, a slight quaver in his voice. Chara felt sorry for the lad, knowing that he couldn't be much older than she was. His youth and inexperience could cost him his young life.

"We don't know whether that is true or not, Phlebius," Galla remonstrated. "Those are only rumors that have been circulated. No one knows much of Britannia. Even I know only what I have been told."

Phlebius shivered. "Imagine sacrificing *humans* to a god.

That's despicable!"

"Is it any different from sacrificing humans for the enjoyment of a mob and calling it entertainment?" Chara asked him softly. "What difference if people are sacrificed to Nero, or some unknown god?"

Decimus tensed beside her, expecting a violent reaction. Instead, the young man looked at her uncomprehendingly a moment before he realized the import of her words. His eyes flickered away and Decimus could have sworn he that he saw guilt written across his features. The boy turned away, rolling over on his mat.

Galla and Trophimus smiled at Chara before they too settled down for the night.

Relaxing back against his own furs, Decimus pulled Chara down into his arms. She curled against him, mumbling into his chest.

"What did you say?"

"I said, I'm sorry."

Decimus was surprised. "You have nothing to be sorry for. What you said was true. And who knows what seeds you may have just planted."

"'I planted the seed, Apollos watered it, but God made it grow,'" she quoted softly. "That's what the Apostle Paul wrote in one of his letters to the church at Corinth. I will have to pray that God sends someone to water my seed."

Decimus gazed at the stars above. The pagans believed their lives and destinies were governed by those pinpricks of light. He was glad he knew that the Maker of the stars controlled his life. And he thanked God with all his heart for bringing this woman into his life.

nine

The weather held for the first three days, though the nights were growing colder the farther they climbed in latitude. The first morning after they left the river behind and entered into the sea, ominous dark clouds began to appear in the northwest. The captain watched them for a long time.

Chara, huddled in her furs, lifted worried eyes to her husband. "Are we in for a storm?"

Decimus glanced down at his shivering wife. If a storm did come, everyone and everything aboard this ship would be soaked within a short period of time. Already Chara's teeth chattered with the cold and damp, And Decimus was beginning to fear that she would become ill.

"It looks that way. Hopefully we can outrun it."

But the storm approached them with incredible speed. As the clouds rolled low over the horizon, the wind began to gain in intensity, causing the sea to heave with its fury.

Chara stared in surprise as the sailors, one by one, began to cut their nails and throw them over the ships rails. When that failed to calm the sea, they started clipping off locks of their hair and doing the same. Regardless of their superstitious entreaties, the storm grew in strength.

Water sprayed over the deck as the ship's bow rose, then crashed into the hollow of the waves. With each plunge of the ship, Chara was thrown mercilessly about on the deck. She noticed that the men were not having the same problem, save Trophimus. Each man seemed to be made from stone as they rolled with the pitch of the ship.

The ship's captain made his way to their side. "We're in for it," he yelled above the increasing wail of the wind. "Take the woman below deck to my quarters, then come back. I'll need every hand on board to help us ride out this gale."

Although it was the middle of the day it seemed more like dusk, the sun hidden behind the thick mass of clouds. Decimus helped Chara to her feet, holding her tightly against his side. They slipped and slid towards the galley entrance. Before going below, Chara saw the men scampering about ship trying to tie everything down. Galla and his soldiers were spreading out to make themselves of use wherever they were needed.

Decimus pushed Chara into the captain's cabin. "Stay here. Whatever you do, don't come on deck unless I tell you to." He could see the fear in her eyes. Reaching out, he pulled her into his arms, kissing the top of her head. "We'll be fine. Remember what you keep telling the rest of us. God is with us."

Releasing her, he strode back up the stairs, taking them two at a time. Clinging to the doorjamb, Chara watched him go. When he was out of sight she closed the door and stumbled across to the captain's bunk. It was nailed down at least, and she clung to it like an anchor as the ship rocked from side to side.

Her fingers grew numb from gripping the wooden bed frame, and she began to shake as the temperature plunged. Her teeth chattered furiously, from both the cold and from fear.

Time passed slowly. Would the storm never end? Chara prayed zealously, hoping the storm would soon spend its energy.

At last, she heard feet in the passageway outside her door. Stumbling across the room, she opened the door. Trophimus was in the corridor, unlashing several ropes from their positions on the walls. He glanced her way briefly.

"What's happening?" Chara yelled above the noise of the storm. Water rushed down the stairs from the open door above, and Chara jumped back, squealing as the cold water soaked her feet.

"It doesn't look good," he yelled back. "We may have to start unloading the cargo to save the ship. You need to. . ."

He stopped as they heard a sound above their heads. A strange creaking sound was followed by a loud crash as one of the masts from topside crashed through the deck and below.

Chara screamed, leaping to safety. Water plunged through the gaping hole left above her, quickly filling the corridor to a depth of several inches.

Trophimus flung himself across the corridor to Chara's side. "Are you all right?"

At her nod, he handed her the ropes in his hands. "Here, take these ropes to Decimus. I have to try and stop the water from coming in. Whatever you do, though, don't go out on the deck. Just hand the rope to someone close to the door."

Chara took the ropes, holding back another scream as more water rushed into the passageway. She struggled to the gangway, clinging to it as she made her way to the top. The door at the top was hanging on its hinges. Water rushed across the deck and down the gangway. Chara clung more tightly to it, not giving an inch.

At the doorway, Chara searched for a familiar face. Everywhere men struggled with the elements. Sailors fought alongside legionnaires, all fighting for their lives.

She finally spotted Decimus a few yards away. He was binding amphoras to the masts with ropes. She yelled but the wind was so fierce it threw her words back at her. Clinging to the gangway with one hand, she began to frantically motion with the ropes in her other. Her arms began to ache with the effort.

The ship plunged into another trough and waves crashed over the side, knocking Decimus from his feet. Chara screamed. Throwing the ropes down, she tried desperately to reach him as he was swept toward the side of the ship.

The mighty ship rose high in the air, then plunged and slammed itself against the water. Chara was thrown off her feet, knocked about like a straw doll. Waves rushed over the sides, pulling at her as they were sucked back to the ocean from whence they came.

Chara managed to lunge for the edge of the gangway, but her grip was tenuous. She clutched frantically with both hands, her fingers digging into the wood posts. She yelled for Decimus, but she knew he could not hear her. Closing her eyes she prayed for his safety.

Oh Lord God, she prayed fervently, *save me! Save us all!*

When the second wave came, Chara's slight strength was no match for it. She was ripped from the gangway, her body hurtling toward the side of the ship. She just managed to grab hold of a piece of rope that was holding an amphora of oil, before the ship rose again on the waves.

What had happened to Decimus? Clinging tightly to the rope with both hands, Chara prayed for help. Through eyes filled with salt water, she saw Decimus pulling himself to his feet. His clothes clung to his body. With one hand he pushed his drenched hair from his eyes.

Then Chara noticed what she hadn't seen before. A rope was tied to Decimus' waist securely holding him to the ships mast. *Thank God!*

Trophimus reached the top of the gangway just in time to see Chara's precarious hold on the rope give way. She slid quickly to the ship's bulwark, her body plastered momentarily to the wood.

Decimus glanced up in time to see Trophimus standing in the stairway, a look of horror upon his face. His eyes flew in the direction the young Roman was looking, and the color suddenly drained from his face.

"Chara!"

Both men lunged toward her at the same time. Decimus was brought up short by the rope around his waist. Clawing frantically at the knot, he watched helplessly as Trophimus was knocked from his feet. A huge wave sucked him toward Chara. Still, he couldn't reach them. If only he had a few more feet of rope.

Trophimus grabbed Chara around the waist, holding tightly as the ship dipped again. They were again plastered to the bulwark. Trophimus knew he had only one chance to save Chara's life. As the ship lifted again, he heaved Chara with all his might toward Decimus.

Decimus had only enough time to grab her tunic before the ship plunged again. Clinging tightly to her garment, they both watched helplessly as Trophimus was slowly sucked over the side of the ship.

"No!"

Chara's scream echoed around the ship, rising above the whine of the wind. Decimus didn't know if the moans he was hearing were coming from his wife or the bansheelike winds.

He managed to get them below, helping Chara to the bunk. Although she clung to him tightly, she stared at him with vacant eyes. Picking her up, he gently lowered her to the bunk.

There was no time to change her clothes. He had to get back topside. He knew he shouldn't leave her, but he had no choice. Teeth chattering, he covered her with a fur blanket, kissed her cold lips, and returned to help fight the storm.

Chara must have slept, for when she awoke fingers of light were piercing the darkness of the cabin. Disoriented, she lifted herself on one elbow, wondering momentarily where she was. Then the events of the night before came crashing down on her like the waves that had pummeled the ship. Moaning, she lay back down, her body racked with sobs.

First Antipus and Agrippina. Now Trophimus. *Dear God! Why? Why?* She remembered Trophimus saying that he felt led to stay with her and Decimus. Had that been God's plan? That Trophimus would lay down his life for hers? She sobbed harder. Dear, dear, Trophimus.

Galla and Decimus found Chara buried beneath a damp fur, crying as though her very heart were breaking. Decimus felt his own heart squeeze tightly within him. What could he do to comfort her? He hadn't been much use when the others had died, so what could he say now?

Deciding that words were useless, he took her in his arms and held her tightly. His eyes found Galla's, and there was sympathy there.

"You better stay with her. My men and I will help the captain repair the ship." He nodded at Chara. "She needs you more."

Decimus pulled Chara with him as he lay back against the bunk. She was no longer sobbing, but her body was tight with tension. He began to stroke her hair gently, murmuring soft words of encouragement. Eventually, he could feel her begin to relax. She lifted her eyes to his, the ravages of her tears plain upon her face.

"It was my fault!"

Decimus stiffened in surprise. "What?"

"I didn't know that you were in no danger. I didn't see the rope around your waist. When I saw you being washed to the side. . ." She buried her face against his chest. "I didn't listen to you or to Trophimus. I went out on the deck."

He was humbled to know that she loved him that much. He sighed, pulling her closer. "It wasn't your fault. It wasn't anyone's fault. It just happened."

"Oh, God!" She moaned, wishing the Lord would take away the picture of Trophimus's face as he was plunging over the side.

Decimus knew that nothing but time would take away the memories. "He saved your life, my love, and he did it because he loved you. Remember that. Think on that."

Chara clung to him more tightly. What if she lost Decimus? It seemed that everyone she loved died. *Dear God, please don't let anything happen to Decimus. Please!*

As Decimus continued to hold her, the hours he had spent fighting the sea began to take their toll. His body relaxed, and soon his breathing told Chara that he was fast asleep. She sighed, snuggling closer. Whatever happened, they still had each other.

❧

It took several days to repair the ship. The mast that had plunged through the deck was split in two and had to be roped together.

The sun shone brightly, a mocking reminder of what they had endured. Many supplies had been washed overboard, but the captain felt they had enough to make it to Britannia without touching those of Rome.

Since temperatures had dropped with the storm and were slow to increase, the captain thought it best if the soldiers, crew, and others made their sleeping quarters in the storage hold. Quarters would be cramped, but a lot better than freezing or sickness.

Decimus worried about Chara. She was lethargic, her eyes dulled with pain. He hadn't realized how much she had loved the young Roman. A twinge of jealousy twisted his insides, but he immediately felt ashamed of himself. What right had he to complain when he withheld his own love from her?

Even now, she leaned against the masthead, huddled in her fur blanket, staring morosely out to sea. Decimus had been unable to reach her with his comfort. He didn't know what else to do.

He watched as Galla approached her, dropping to a squatting position. Decimus could see the soldier talking, but Chara continued to stare ahead. Finally something Galla said seemed to penetrate the fog of her grief. Turning her face to him, she shook her head at whatever he had said. They talked for some time before Galla reached out and cupped her cheek with his hand, then rose to his feet.

Decimus watched as Galla crossed the deck, drawing up beside him. His eyes went beyond the Roman to where Chara sat, a look of peace on her face for the first time in days.

"What did you say to her?"

Galla shrugged. "I merely reminded her that Trophimus did exactly what the Lord had done for us. He gave his life for someone he loved." His eyes went over Decimus before he turned, leaning on the bulwark. "I also reminded her that she was trying to do the same thing. I asked her if she would have wanted you to feel guilty if she had died trying to help you."

"She very well could have!" Decimus choked, his heart thudding at the possibility.

"But she didn't. Have you told her that you love her?"

Decimus shook his head, not bothering to deny it. "No. There doesn't seem to be a right time."

"There almost wasn't *any* time," Galla told him roughly. "What if she had been washed overboard?"

Decimus felt his heart sink. Even the thought of it nearly drove him mad.

Galla squeezed his shoulder. "Don't wait *too* long, my friend. There may never be a *right* time, but there could very well be *no* time."

Decimus watched him walk away, making his way toward the captain. His eyes went back to Chara. She was sitting there trying to soak in what little sunshine she could, her eyes closed, her head thrown back. Decimus clutched the bulwark tighter. He stood a long time thus. Sighing, he turned and went below.

Chara opened her eyes and watched Decimus leave, her heart heavy within her. If only she could believe Galla when he told her that Decimus loved her. But Decimus, though he was gentle and kind, was definitely not loving. He had comforted her as he would have comforted a child.

She sighed, watching the gulls flying overhead. A good omen, the sailors said. But not for Trophimus. Galla was right, she knew. Trophimus wouldn't have wanted her to feel guilty at his loss, but still it was hard.

Trophimus had given his life for her, and Jesus had, too. If she felt guilty because of Trophimus, how much more so should she feel guilty because of her Lord. Jesus would have died for her had she been the only human being on earth. What had He done to deserve to die? The same as Trophimus. He loved her more than His own life.

Trophimus would forgive her, just as her Lord had. Jesus didn't want her to feel guilty, He wanted her to feel *loved*. She bowed her head, giving her burden over to her Master.

The remainder of their voyage was uneventful. The sea's peaceful serenity mirrored Chara's. Once she had given her guilt over to God, peace had come.

The sun shone weakly on the surface of the water, giving it a glassy appearance. Chara watched as schools of fish rose to the surface, flying along through the water as though racing the big ship. She laughed aloud at the thought, wishing them well in their endeavor.

Decimus, coming upon her at that moment, smiled at her laughter. It seemed as if it had been such a long time since he had heard it. He leaned against the bulwark, looking at her seriously. "It's good to hear you laugh."

She didn't turn to him, but seemed to be contemplating something in the distance. "You know, the farther we get from Rome, the lighter my heart feels."

Decimus frowned. The closer they got to Britannia, the more uneasy he became. "Are we ever really free from Rome?" He didn't really expect an answer.

When she turned to him, the look in her eyes sent chills racing down his spine. Her look was distant, as though seeing into the future. "I feel like we are on the edge of destiny, and that you and I will have a part in changing that destiny."

"What do you mean?"

"We have the opportunity to preach the Word to a people who have never heard it taught before," she mused. "At least not that we know of."

Biting his lip, Decimus took her hands into his. Hers were like ice and he began to absently rub them between his own. "That may be a whole lot more dangerous than anything we have experienced thus far."

"Perhaps," she answered softly. "But you can only lose your life once. Jesus died for me, I will gladly do the same for Him."

Decimus pushed back from the bulwark. He didn't want to frighten her, but Britannia was far from the civilization she knew. Its people still lived in tribes, and from the accounts he had heard, they were far fiercer than anything the Romans had introduced. He knew that the wilds of Gaul were very similar to Britannia—but Chara had lived in a city, surrounded by civilization. She had never been exposed to the Druids' religion and he wondered if she would be able to even comprehend the cruelty of human sacrifice.

Remembering the blood-soaked sands of the arenas of Rome, he decided that on second thought perhaps the Britons and Romans were more alike than he had at first thought. At least the Britons were fighting for their lives, their homes. They didn't kill on a whim. Not from what he remembered, which honestly was not much. But Chara was strong, he knew, stronger than he sometimes thought; certainly her faith in God was even sturdier than his own, and with that behind her, perhaps she would be able to withstand anything.

Chara smiled, reaching up a hand and gently cupping his cheek. "You needn't fear for me, Decimus. And no matter what happens, I wish to be right by your side."

Decimus shook his head, an answering smile appearing on his face. "Galla might have something to say about that."

"Galla is not my husband, nor is he my master. Only you are both."

"No, my love, I am not your master. You and I share the same Master." He pulled her into his arms, enfolding her in his warm embrace. "We will serve Him together, come what may."

They stood watching as the sun began to dip below the horizon. Before long the moon replaced the sun's light with its own bright orb, its reflection sending a shimmering path across the water to the ship.

Chara wanted the moment to last forever, but eventually the cold drove them inside. Decimus helped her prepare a pallet as far from the others as possible. Chara lay down, one eyebrow winging upwards as Decimus turned to leave.

"Are you not coming to bed?"

Decimus shook his head. "No. Galla and I have much to

discuss. According to the captain, we should reach the shores of Britannia by morning."

"What do you think we'll find there?"

He would have reassured her if he could. The problem was, he couldn't. He had no idea how Galla would extricate them from the company they seemed to find themselves in. Decimus had no desire to spend any more time with Caltupa than was absolutely necessary.

"I guess we'll find out when we get there."

Decimus crossed to where Galla awaited him. They seated themselves far away from the others, lowering their voices so as not to be heard.

"We should reach the southern coast of Britannia tomorrow," Galla told Decimus. "Caltupa will probably tell me what orders he received when we reach there. As of yet, I have no idea what has been planned. Caltupa has been very close mouthed. I assume his orders were to wait until we reached Britannia and he heard the reports from Rome's spies."

Decimus leaned back against the rough planks of the ship. "Chara certainly can't march into Britannia with your troops. What can we do?"

Galla expelled his breath slowly. "I don't know. I hadn't planned on having Roman company on this trip."

"What will you do if your orders are to lead Caltupa and his men against the Britons?"

Galla shook his head. "Let's not borrow trouble. I don't think that will happen."

"What if it turns into a full-scale war?" The thought had Decimus' stomach roiling. How could the people of Britannia withstand another siege by the Roman war machine? Soldiers who had fought there told humorous stories of farmers who went to battle against the seasoned Roman troops with nothing but long, slashing swords and no armor. They depended upon their speed to try and outmaneuver the Roman troops. Many men had died impaled by Roman javelins.

Galla's voice dropped even lower. "My concern is not

whether I will be forced to go into battle with the troops. I am in a dilemma as to what to do about you and Chara."

Decimus glanced at his wife curled against the ship's timber. Her chest rose and fell softly, assuring him that she was fast asleep. "She's been through a lot," he told Galla softly.

Nodding, Galla got to his feet. "And now, my friend, it is time for us to sleep as well, for on the morrow I believe we will have a lot more to go through." Reaching down, Galla helped Decimus to his feet. "I take it you still have not found the right time?"

Irritated, Decimus shook his head. Galla watched him a full minute before turning and without a word striding to his sleeping mat in the corner.

Decimus crawled beneath the fur with Chara, for the first time aware that his teeth were chattering. In her sleep, Chara turned and curled herself against him. Slowly, his teeth stopped chattering. As warmth spread through him, he closed his eyes and began to pray. His petitions were short and to the point. Within minutes he was fast asleep.

ten

"Centurion."

Galla looked up at the man standing next to him as he low-ered the rope he was holding to the deck beside him. Caltupa's face was rigid, his features betraying nothing of his thoughts. He certainly hadn't taken long to make his presence known. The ship had docked only moments before.

"You have orders for me, captain?"

"Aye, centurion."

Galla rose to his full height, which was several inches taller than the captain. His eyes betrayed nothing of the trepidation that was inching its way along his midsection.

Caltupa held out a long leather cylinder and Galla took it. His eyebrows flew upwards as he recognized the seal. Caesar's.

Several things ran through Galla's mind, not least of which was whether Captain Caltupa was aware of what was in the document. Since both the container and the scroll were sealed, Galla felt fairly certain that the contents were some-thing which he would not care to deal with.

His eyes met Caltupa's. "You know what this document contains?"

"No, my lord. I was told merely that if anything happened to you on the way here, that I was to burn the pouch and it's contents. Unopened."

"I see." Galla absently tapped the pouch against his hand. "I'll read this in the captain's quarters."

As he turned to leave, Caltupa put a restraining hand on his arm. "My orders are to wait for you to read the discharge and then to burn it."

Galla was surprised, his curiosity growing. "Very well, come with me then."

Galla opened the scroll after they were safely in the captain's cabin. His eyes grew wide, the color disappearing from his ruddy face. Slowly his eyes met Caltupa's. The captain stared at him impassively.

"You know nothing of what's in this discharge? You are certain?"

The captain snapped to attention, slapping a salute. "On my honor, centurion. I have not read the parchment. As you can see, the seal was intact."

Galla nodded slowly. He handed the scroll to the captain. "Carry out your orders then."

With Galla watching, the captain strode across the small room and placed the parchment in the burning brazier. As the flames licked at the paper, Galla watched mesmerized. Thoughts were swirling swiftly through his mind and he was trying to sort them into order.

"Centurion, I was told that you would have orders for me."

Galla sighed. "Your orders are to head north, as far as Londinium. You, the troops, and the supplies. You are to meet up with several other contingents awaiting your arrival."

"And you?"

"I will not be going with you."

Caltupa's eyes narrowed, but he said nothing. He hadn't seen the scroll, therefore he knew nothing of the orders it contained. The only thing he knew for certain was that he didn't trust the centurion. He couldn't say why exactly, it was just a feeling he had. For one thing he treated his slaves more like friends than servants. It didn't make sense to him, but he knew better than to argue. If the centurion was lying, he would find out once he reached Londinium, and *if* he was lying, then may the gods help him, because Caltupa would not hesitate to track him down and have him crucified.

Galla turned and left the scowling captain standing alone in the center of the room.

ह

Decimus finished tying their furs into a bundle, securing the knot tightly. Chara sat on the deck surrounded by piles and packs. She lifted worried eyes to her husband.

"What do you think will happen now?"

Decimus shrugged. "We'll have to wait and see what Galla's orders are. Whatever happens, God is with us." He wasn't nearly as confident as he led Chara to believe. If Galla had to lead an expedition into Britannia, Decimus knew they would have to part company. He would have to take Chara and flee. Glancing around at the ship's crew hurrying to and fro, he decided that wouldn't be too hard to accomplish.

He frowned as Galla strode across the deck toward them, his face a study in contradictions. His forehead was creased in a frown, yet there was a small smile on his face.

"You have your orders?" Decimus asked.

Galla nodded. "Yes, and with them an answer to prayer."

Chara stood up and came to their side. They waited for Galla to continue, curious as to how orders from Rome could be an answer to anyone's prayers.

Galla lowered his voice. "My orders are to proceed north and locate my grandfather's tribe. Nero knows that my grandfather was an influential man. I'm supposed to try and convince them to ally themselves with Rome against the other tribes."

Decimus glowered. "How is this an answer to prayer? Tribe betraying tribe?"

Grinning, Galla reached down and started lifting packs from the deck. "I'm supposed to go alone. Caltupa is to proceed to Londinium to meet up with other Roman troops that are waiting there."

"And what of us?" Chara asked the question Decimus was thinking.

Galla straightened. "You'll come with me, of course."

Chara frowned. "But you just said that you were to go alone."

Suddenly comprehending the turn of their thoughts, Galla laughed. "I'm sorry. I meant no other troops will attend me. Only my slaves."

Decimus sighed with relief. He began to help Galla lift their packs and followed him down the plank to the dock.

"Wait here," Galla told them. "I'll see about our horses."

Before long the ship was unloaded and Galla had their things removed from the others. "Fortunately, we bought these horses with our own money, or we would be walking. As it is, I had to pry them from Caltupa."

"What do we do now?" Decimus asked, lifting Chara to her horse.

"I had intended to stay in town, but I think it best if we put some distance between us and this fair city."

Chara looked around curiously. "Why?"

"It seems that hostility toward Romans is growing. Since Queen Boudicca of the Iceni tribe was killed several years ago and her daughters raped, a few of her followers have mounted another effort against the Romans. They are trying to rout any and every Roman in Britannia. They are even killing anyone considered to be a Roman sympathizer."

Chara paled. "But what has that to do with staying in the city?"

"Local tribes have been burning cities they think are necessary to the Romans." Galla smiled wryly. "Obviously, this city would be a great target."

"But couldn't we stay the night? Chara is tired. It's been a long voyage."

Galla shook his head. "No, I think not. One of the dock managers sympathetic to Rome tells me that there are rumors of a raiding party in the vicinity."

"All the more reason to stay here," Decimus told him.

Again Galla shook his head. "If they come, it will be for one purpose. We can't take that chance. I think it would be safer farther inland."

"And if we meet them on the road?"

Galla smiled. "I have thought of that. Come, we have much to do."

ta

Later, Chara studied Galla on his lead horse. He was an

impressive man in the uniform of the Roman soldier, but he was equally impressive in the warrior uniform of the southern tribesmen. His yellow brown tunic, or *pais* as the Britons called it, hung midway between his thighs and his knees. A broadsword was affixed to his waist on a belt, tucking the pais in and giving it a fitted appearance.

The one piece of attire that seemed to give both Galla and Decimus some problems was the llawdyr, wrapped closely around their thighs and legs. Chara grinned as she noticed Decimus shift again in his saddle. Obviously, the pants took some getting used to.

Galla's sagum was draped around his shoulders, providing warmth from the autumn chill. Although Galla's was checkered, the predominant color being red, Decimus had chosen one of sky blue, dyed from the woad plant.

The thought crossed Chara's mind that she would have been more comfortable in the same garb, but since this was men's clothing, and warriors' at that, she had settled for a long woolen pais. She was still enthralled with the checkered pattern of the material. Blues, yellows, reds, and oranges vied for prominence in the garment. The colors were somewhat loud, so she had chosen a brown sagum to go with it. The mantle was made from thick sheep's wool and she snuggled deeply into its folds.

As they traveled, the sun began to move toward its zenith, though the rays were tepid at best. Chara felt herself beginning to nod in the saddle. Jerking herself upright, she concentrated on the steam coming from her horse's nostrils. The steady clop, clop of the horses' hooves, however, began to lull her to sleep again.

Decimus heard a soft thud behind him. Turning, his heart lurched into his throat at the sight of Chara lying beneath the hooves of her mount. Fortunately, the beast was so well trained, it remained absolutely immobile.

"Galla!"

Decimus didn't wait for an answer. Flinging himself from

his horse, he rushed to Chara's side. She was sitting up, rubbing her hip.

"Are you hurt?"

Shaking her head, Chara started to rise. "I don't think so. Only my pride." When she tried to stand, she fell back to her knees with a cry of pain.

Decimus was on his knees in an instant, lifting her foot. Gently, he tried to turn it. At Chara's soft gasp, he stopped.

"What happened?" Galla bent over them, watching Decimus lower Chara's foot gently to the ground.

"Chara has hurt her ankle. I don't think anything is broken. It looks like a bad sprain though."

Already Chara's foot was beginning to turn slightly blue. Decimus reached down and lifted her into his arms. As gently as possible, he settled her back on her horse, but no matter how gentle he was, he could tell she was in excruciating pain.

"More than your foot is hurt."

"I think perhaps you are right," she answered him softly, her lips beginning to tremble.

Galla turned around slowly, surveying the countryside around them. "Wait here," he told them.

They watched as Galla was swallowed up by the forest. Decimus took a fur and spread it on the ground.

"Come," he told Chara, reaching his arms for her. "You'll be more comfortable lying down."

Chara slid carefully into his arms, wincing at the pain that ran through her body. More than likely she was just very bruised. How heavenly it would be to soak in a hot bath and then go to sleep.

Decimus carefully put her on the fur, then sat down beside her. "Are you sure you're all right?"

"I think so."

As Decimus had predicted, it did feel better to lie down, and before long Chara drifted off to sleep. Decimus kept a sharp lookout. He was beginning to worry at Galla's absence. What was taking him so long?

Decimus finally spotted Galla returning. Decimus grinned. If not for the hair, Galla could easily be mistaken for a Briton. Although most Britons had conformed to the style of the Romans, many were returning to the longer hairstyle of earlier tribesmen. Decimus suspected it was more as a way of throwing off any Roman influence, than because it was more preferred.

Galla knelt beside Chara, his eyes softening as he watched her sleep. "How is she?"

"She doesn't complain, but I think she's pretty bruised."

Galla rose to his feet. "Let her sleep a while. I've found a cave through the trees and slightly up that hill there." Decimus followed his pointing finger. "There's a place where we can keep the horses, too. As you can see, it's pretty well hidden from the road."

"What then?"

"I think Chara will need to rest a few days, give her body time to heal." Galla paused, staring off into the distance. "You'll be safe there for a while. I'll leave provisions with you and there's a stream nearby where you can get water."

Decimus rose quickly to his feet. "What do you intend to do?"

"I'm going to investigate the countryside."

"What? Are you out of your mind? What if something happens to you? What do we do then? How will we even know?"

Galla smiled wryly. "Calm down. If I'm not back in three days. . ."

Decimus' eyes flashed fire. "What? What should I do then?"

Galla took a moment to answer. When he did, his eyes were serious. "You must go on."

Decimus shoved his hands back through his hair, expelling his breath angrily. "This is crazy. We should stick together."

"Decimus." Galla's quiet voice stopped Decimus from pacing like an angry lion. "Look to the north. Feel the air."

A thin dark line was spread across the horizon, and although it was still afternoon, the temperatures were beginning to drop.

"A storm?"

Galla shook his head. "More than a storm. The beginning of winter. When this storm passes, winter will set in with a vengeance. We can't stay in a cave. We have to find a village or town."

"But if you get caught out in that. . ."

"That's why I said three days. I'm predicting the storm won't start for at least three days. I hope to be back by then."

Realizing they could do nothing else, Decimus sighed. "Very well, but I don't like it."

"That makes two of us."

Decimus bent to gather Chara into his arms. Her eyes opened briefly, then flickered closed again.

"I hope she stays asleep," Decimus told Galla. "She won't feel the pain that way."

Galla nodded. "The cave is not far. Do you think you can carry her?"

Decimus smiled down into Chara's sleeping face. "She weighs little more than a feather."

By the time they reached the cave, Decimus had altered his opinion. Although Chara was light, after two miles she became a weight in his arms. Finally, they reached the cave, and Decimus breathed a sigh of relief. He followed Galla inside and saw why Galla had taken so long to return. A stack of wood lay at the back of the cave near a dark tunnel that led farther into the cavern.

Galla spread the furs on the floor, making a pallet for Decimus to lay Chara on. When he put her down, she opened her eyes. Blinking up at him sleepily, she smiled. "Is it morning?"

Galla and Decimus burst into laughter. At her puzzled look, Galla turned to go outside. "I'll bring in the rest of the things. You explain to our sleeping beauty here what we've decided."

Chara didn't like their plan, but neither was she in any position to argue. Every time she tried to move, pain sliced through her body. Finally, she lay back and stared up at the ceiling of the cave.

Decimus had already started a fire and the flames caused fingers of light to swirl eerily on the rock walls. Chara watched their dancing patterns as she listened to Decimus and Galla finalizing their plans. She prayed for Galla and his safety.

When Galla knelt beside her, she smiled slightly at his worried expression. She took one of his hands into her own. "I'll be fine," she told him reassuringly. "It's you I'm concerned about."

He grinned. "I'm not the one inclined to fall off horses."

She wrinkled her nose at him. "No, you're the one who would drive others until *they* did."

Galla stopped smiling. "Chara, I am so sorry. You are right. If not for my pigheadedness none of this would have happened."

"No!" Chara tried to rise. Crying out in pain, she slid back to the furs. "I was only teasing. Please don't feel that it was your fault!"

"She's right," Decimus told him. "We could have refused to agree with you, but we thought you were right. Don't start second-guessing yourself now."

Galla didn't look convinced.

"Remember, Galla," Chara told him. "Everything that has happened so far and continues to happen in the future is according to God's will. You reminded me of that when Trophimus died."

He touched her cheek briefly, a wry smile twisting his lips. Rising to his feet, he turned to Decimus. "Take care of our girl. You should have time to tell her something."

Decimus frowned, his eyes sending messages to the Roman that made Galla grin. He lifted a small pack and threw it over his shoulders, then fixed Decimus with a steely eye. "Remember, three days."

Decimus watched Galla wend his way down the hill. He looked back once and waved, then he was gone from sight. Decimus felt a powerful sense of loss and realized that he had come to depend on the soldier. Looking to the north he saw that the ominous dark line was still there. He hoped Galla was right about it not reaching their location for three days. He offered up a prayer for Galla's safety, then returned to the cave.

Chara lay as he had left her, staring up at the ceiling of the cave. She turned her head when he entered.

"What did Galla mean when he said you could tell me something?"

Decimus shrugged. "Who knows what that crazy Roman has on his mind?" He put more wood on the fire, refusing to look in Chara's direction. Although she knew he was keeping something back, she didn't press him. He would tell her whatever was on his mind when he thought it necessary.

Although the temperatures had dropped to freezing, their shelter was relatively warm. Chara would have preferred less smoke, but she was thankful not to be spending the night in a tent.

Darkness descended quickly, another sure sign of winter. Decimus rummaged through their supplies to get them a meal. He brought Chara hers and helped her sit up, propping her against the wall.

She flinched, but she didn't cry out. Every bone in her body felt as if it were bruised, but she knew she would probably be a lot sorer tomorrow.

When they settled down for the night, Decimus was careful to stay close enough to share his warmth, but far enough away not to hurt her. Chara missed the security of his arms around her. Her last waking thought was of Galla.

❧

Galla paused beside a stream, dipping his hands in and drinking thirstily. He scanned the forest around him, listening for sounds of life. None were present. He frowned. There should be forest sounds: birds, frogs, something.

The hair on the back of his neck prickled in warning. Turning, he had no time to draw his sword before something smashed against his head.

eleven

Galla awakened slowly, his head throbbing. Moaning, he tried to open his eyes but they were too heavy, as though a bronze weight were holding them down.

He tried to remember what had happened, but his mind was still fuzzy. He lay still, letting consciousness slowly return to him. As he lay there, he became aware of whispered voices in the room. They were speaking the language his father and grandfather had taught him as a child.

"Why did you have to bring him here?"

Although the words were whispered and low, Galla could tell that the voice was that of a woman. An angry woman at that.

"What could I do, Mother? I couldn't leave him there to die!"

The owner of the second voice was obviously young. A boy. If he was the one who had struck the blow, Rome would do well to have such in their legions.

A long silence was followed by a soft sigh. "I suppose not. But Cadvan, only you would have the audacity to try to kill someone and then bring him home for me to take care of."

Galla opened his eyes. Slowly his vision came into focus. The first thing he noticed was that they were in a cave, but one that was much more homelike than the one where he had left Decimus and Chara. Obviously, someone had taken pains to make this a home.

Turning his head in the direction of the voices, he noticed a young boy, about thirteen or fourteen, standing before a woman, his head bent. He was tall, his skin dark, his hair as black as the midnight sky. He was a handsome lad.

The woman was so opposite from him in looks that Galla

could only stare. She was tall for a woman, but her skin was as creamy as ivory, her hair yellow and as pale as the moonlight. She was neither young, nor old. She seemed close to Galla's age, but her face wore the look of having seen much of life.

Feeling eyes on her, she turned to Galla. Her ice blue eyes were cold, distant. She came across the room and looked down at him lying on the mat.

"So, you're awake."

Galla tried to rise but found himself unable. Looking down, he saw he was tied with ropes. He looked to the woman for an explanation. Instead, she turned and went back to her son.

"Did you make sure you left no tracks to follow?"

"I made sure. Not even Cadwaladyr could track me this time."

The woman smiled at the pride in her son's voice, her eyes softening. "Go now. Make sure he was alone." Lifting a quiver of arrows and a bow from beside the entrance to the cave, she handed them to the boy. "Cadvan, deer would be nice for supper."

The boy's chest swelled with pride at her confidence in him. Nodding, he turned and left.

The woman returned to Galla, fixing him with a cold gaze. "What is your name, and what tribe are you from?"

Galla was hesitant to answer her, but he knew he couldn't lie. "My name is Galla. I am from the Trinovantes."

If anything, her eyes grew colder. Galla almost shivered under their intense look. "Where am I?" he ventured to ask.

The woman studied him for a long time, and Galla took the time to study her in return. She was a beautiful woman. Never had he seen hair such color. Even Chara's was a much brighter blond. This woman's was almost silver.

"I'll ask the questions," she informed him, and Galla felt himself bristle at the woman's arrogance. He might be trussed up like a pheasant, but he knew ways to free himself. He smiled slightly as he considered the look on his captor's face if he should choose to do so. Right now, though, he needed time to regain his strength.

The woman watched him silently. Her heart skipped a beat when she saw his eyes darken, a slow smile spreading across his face. She felt a thrill of fear for the first time in years. He looked so much like. . .

Her mind shied away from such futile thoughts. Reaching down, she gave the ropes a tug to check their security. Satisfied, she leaned back. "Why is a Trinovante traveling alone through Cantiaci land?"

Again Galla hesitated. A voice seemed to whisper in his mind to tell the woman the truth. Still. . .

"I am looking for the Trinovantes. I have just arrived from Rome."

She jerked back as though he had struck her, her eyes going wide. "You're a *Roman!*" She almost hissed the words.

Galla nodded. The motion sent a wrenching pain slicing through his head. Closing his eyes tightly, he fought the bile rising in his throat. He gritted his teeth until the nausea slowly subsided.

When he opened his eyes again, the woman was gone.

&

Decimus looked up at the sky for what must have been the hundredth time. The storm was moving closer, but Galla had been right. Two days had passed and the storm was still a good distance away. He turned and went back to where Chara was sitting on the furs.

"Still no sign of Galla?"

Decimus shook his head. "No, but he said three days, so I don't really expect him back before tomorrow." He sat down next to her. "How are you feeling?"

She smiled slightly. "My ankle still hurts, but the rest of me seems to be healing. I'm just a little stiff."

Positioning himself behind her, Decimus began to gently knead her shoulders. Chara dropped her head forward, closing her eyes.

"That feels good," she murmured.

For a moment, Decimus' hands stilled, then he started rubbing again. Swallowing hard, he soon realized that this was a big mistake. The very smell of her stirred his senses. Abruptly, he stood and walked back to the entrance to the cave.

Chara stared at him, mystified. What had she done now? Every time she thought they were growing closer, Decimus pulled himself away. What was he so afraid of? She frowned. Perhaps he knew that she loved him and he wanted to make certain she understood that he didn't feel the same way. Did his heart belong to another? In the beginning she had thought so, but now. . .now she wasn't so sure.

He had called her "my love" for some time now, ever since they were married, but she knew that had been for the soldiers' benefit. How did he really feel about her? If only she could really be his love. If only he would look at her with eyes of love when he said it. Lately, the words had become just a habit with him.

Getting up, she slowly made her way to his side. Laying her hand on his arm, she felt him tense.

"What is it, Decimus? Did I do something wrong?"

He didn't look at her for a long time. Finally, he sighed. Turning to her, he looked deep into her eyes. That was his first mistake. The second was not looking away when he had the chance. Now it was too late. He was hypnotized by the luminous glow emanating from the depths of her soft, brown eyes.

"Chara. . ." Whatever he had been about to say was lost to the moment. Bending forward, he pressed his lips to hers.

Chara reached up, curling her arms about his neck, pressing herself closer. Decimus wrapped his arms about her slender body, pulling her tightly into his embrace. He pulled back for a moment, staring intently into her eyes. The soft light of love answered the question he had been about to ask. Still, he had time to turn back.

A fire began to burn within him, slowly affecting his reason. Seeing his hesitation, Chara pulled his head back down to hers. "Please, Decimus," she whispered against his lips.

Lifting her into his arms, Decimus made his way back to the

furs. He laid her against them, then joined her on their softness. There was no turning back now.

❧

Galla watched the opening to the cave for a long while. Finally, the woman returned.

"Is there a reason I'm being held prisoner?" Galla asked.

She ignored him. Going about her business, she fed more wood to the brazier she used for light. Galla watched her as she pulled a basket of woolen yarn over to a loom and began to weave.

"My lady," he said softly, "could you not tell me what crime I have committed? Could you not at least tell me your name?"

He watched her shoulders slump; her fingers stilled their movement, but still she didn't turn around. After what seemed a long while, her voice came quietly across the room. "My name is Eudemia."

Galla frowned. Where had he heard that name before? It was an elusive memory, one that hovered on the edge of his consciousness.

"I mean you no harm," he continued softly.

"Romans mean nothing else," she spit at him.

Galla tried again. "It is true, I am a Roman, but my father was Trinovante, as was my grandfather."

She turned on her stool. "That endears you to me no more than being a Roman."

Curious, Galla studied the woman. "Do you not belong to one of the tribes?"

Her lip curled derisively. "I claim no tribe." She turned back and began weaving again.

Galla glanced around him. It was hard to believe that this was a cave, so homelike had she made it. But why did she live in a cave?

"Do you and your son live alone here?"

"You certainly are a pushy-nosed one." He could hear the amusement in her voice.

Galla thought about it. Yes, he supposed he was inquisitive, but the woman intrigued him. Why would a beautiful woman live alone with her son in a cave? And why did she say she claimed no tribe? He didn't miss the fact that she had said she didn't *claim* one, not that she didn't belong to one. Sometimes it helped to surprise an answer from someone, so Galla decided to put his thoughts into a question.

"Why would a beautiful woman choose to live alone in a cave? Have you no family?"

She glared at him angrily. "Don't call me beautiful."

Surprised, Galla decided not to answer her. Instead, she got up from the stool and came to him. She knelt down beside him, her look intense.

"What are you doing here, Roman?"

For some reason, Galla felt he could trust her. He paused only a moment before he told her his story. The only part he left out was about Chara and Decimus. Better that she not know of their whereabouts. If anyone was going to die, let it be him.

When he finished, her lips curled derisively. "And you expect me to believe that a *Roman* has come all the way to Britannia to tell others about a *Jewish* God."

"He is not a Jewish God. He is everyone's God."

"So you say." Getting up, she went back to her work, her back once more to him. "I have no time for gods. Nor do I have any desire to worship any."

Galla lay there a long time, trying to decide what to do next. Eudemia turned on her stool. "What does your god ask in the way of sacrifices?"

Galla's eyebrows flew up. He took his time before answering, realizing that this was no idle question. "He asks for no sacrifices, only your life."

Her eyes widened. "You must give up your life? I'm surprised anyone would choose to serve such a god." She continued to regard him curiously. "How old must you be before you surrender your life?"

Frowning, Galla tried to reason out her thinking. "Any age is permissible. Even the young can believe."

Her eyes grew cold again. "Young as in my son's age?"

Galla had no idea what had caused such an abrupt change in the woman's demeanor. "I know boys his age that choose to serve God. Girls, too."

"And you? How old have you decided to be before you give your life to this god of yours?" she snarled.

Galla was really confused now. "I have already given my life to my Lord," he answered softly.

Her eyes went slowly over him, returning to his face. Her eyebrows rose slowly upward. "You seem in perfect health for a dead man."

Suddenly comprehending the turn of her thoughts, Galla smiled slightly. "When I say 'give my life to the Lord,' I mean I will serve Him all the days of my life. I would die for Him if necessary, but He does not require human sacrifices. He no longer even asks for animal sacrifices, because His own Son was sacrificed for all."

Puzzled, she came back and knelt beside him again. "His son was sacrificed? If He were a god, how could He allow this?"

Galla pressed his lips together. How could he make her understand? Deciding that it would be best to start at the beginning, Galla unfolded the Lord's plan of salvation to her.

When he finished, Eudemia was staring over his head, lost in thought. She could not comprehend such love. Give her son to save another? No, it was beyond her imagination.

Cadvan came through the entrance, a young fallow deer slung over his shoulder. He looked at his mother sitting so close to the man and frowned.

"Is something wrong, Mother?"

She rose gracefully to her feet. "No, son." Tears formed in her eyes as she watched her boy. Galla's words were fresh in her mind. Going to her son's side, she hugged him tightly.

He pulled back slightly, puzzled. "Mother?"

Smiling, she stroked a hand down his cheek. "Sorry. Dress the meat, will you?"

"What about him?" Cadvan shrugged his shoulders in

Galla's direction.

"I don't know yet. Go dress the meat."

When the boy left the cave, Eudemia turned to Galla. "You have an unusual god. Maybe you could tell me more about Him sometime."

"If you would free me, perhaps I could help with your work."

She glowered at him. "I didn't say I believed you. No, Roman, I am still unsure what to do about you."

Cadvan came back into the cave. "There's a winter storm approaching. I'd say two days away."

He handed his mother the meat and she took it to a table and began cutting it into chunks. "Get me some vegetables to go with this."

Galla watched the two as they prepared their meal and went about preparing for the night. What was to become of him? More than that, what day was this? His thoughts on Chara and Decimus, Galla began to wiggle the ropes. He had to get back.

Eudemia brought him a bowl of stew. Kneeling down beside him, she began to feed it into his mouth a little at a time. Galla chewed slowly, all the while watching the woman. Where had he seen eyes like that before? There was something vaguely familiar about Eudemia. And what of her son? His coloring was more the coloring of the Mediterranean region than of Britannia. What was their story? He was more than a little curious.

"You need to rest tonight. Tomorrow, we'll decide what's to be done about you."

Cadvan came and stood beside her. "I'm sorry, Mother. I wasn't thinking. At first I meant to kill him, but. . ."

Reaching up, Eudemia took his hand into hers, rubbing it against her cheek. "Don't be sorry, my son. You are not a killer. I am proud of you."

He frowned at her. "But what if he is from Cadwaladyr?"

Galla glanced from one to the other. "Is Cadwaladyr another tribe?"

Eudemia grinned. "He probably wishes it were so. His own tribe. Yes, I could see Cadwaladyr strutting to such a tune."

"I know nothing of this Cadwaladyr," Galla told them. "I am only here to try and find my father's tribe."

"Perhaps," Eudemia agreed. "But for now, let us get some sleep." She rose and went to snuff out the oil pots. Darkness filled the cave, save for the light from the brazier. The cave was still comfortably warm, and Galla noticed the furs covering the entrance to keep out the cold.

That was a good idea. He hoped Decimus would think to do the same.

&

Decimus leaned over Chara, stroking the hair from her face with his fingers. She smiled dreamily up at him.

"What are you thinking?" he asked her softly.

She answered him just as softly. "How much I love you."

Frowning, Decimus sat up, turning his back to her. Chara began to run her fingers lightly over the scars on his bare skin and he shuddered.

"What is wrong, Decimus? Have I displeased you?"

Decimus shoved his hands back forcefully through his unruly gold locks. Had she displeased him? Never! In her innocence, she had pleased him more than he could have imagined. She was soft and gentle, loving and kind. Expelling his breath in a harsh breath, he threw himself back against the furs. He rubbed his face with his hands.

"What if you get pregnant, Chara?"

She frowned down at him. "You don't wish to have children?" The thought had never occurred to her, and it hurt her now. She loved children and had hoped for a big family.

Reaching up, he pulled her down onto his chest. His hand slid around her neck and he began to stroke her silky skin. Chara felt her heart begin to pound.

"My love," he told her. "It's not having the children, it's having the children *here*."

Chara suddenly sobered. She had given no thought whatever to their circumstances. She smiled ruefully. She thought mainly with her heart. So sure was she of Decimus' protection, so secure was she in his ability to care for her, she had given no thought to an uncertain future.

As Decimus continued to stroke his fingers down her back, Chara's eyes became liquid pools.

"Don't look at me like that," Decimus warned her huskily.

She lay on his chest, propping her cheeks on her balled fists. "I love you, Decimus, for now and for always. And I believe God will take care of us."

"Like Trophimus?"

Chara frowned. "Are you beginning to doubt? Trophimus is in God's hands. No power on earth can take him away from the love of God. Just as no power on earth can separate *us* from Him." She placed her hands on the ground on either side of his head. "Someday, someone may separate us from each other, but they can never separate us from God. Satan is trying to weed you out, beloved. Don't let him do it."

Decimus wrapped his arms around her waist, smiling into her serious eyes. "So wise for someone so young. You are beautiful."

She flushed hotly and would have pulled away, but Decimus held her firmly.

"You *are* beautiful, inside and out. I thank God for you every day. I love you, Chara. I think I have from the moment I laid eyes on you."

Tears welled in her eyes at the unexpected admission. One spilled over and dripped down her cheek. Decimus watched her, not sure what had made her cry. Suddenly, he felt very uncertain.

"I didn't mean to make you cry."

She smiled then. "Tears of joy. I never thought any man would say such things to me. Oh, Decimus, I love you, too."

She bent to kiss him on the mouth. He rolled over, taking her with him. Neither one heard the wind begin to howl outside. Neither one noticed when the fire died down. Neither one noticed when darkness descended.

twelve

Decimus knelt beside the stream, filling the goatskin flask with icy water. His mind was not on what he was doing. Three days had passed, and they still had seen no sign of Galla. Decimus had no idea what he would do if Galla didn't return. Although Chara's foot had healed to a point where she could limp on it, she still couldn't travel far.

Suddenly his arms were seized in an ironlike grip from behind. He was pulled back from the stream and spun around. Two men held him fast in their tight grip, his arms twisted behind his back. He struggled a moment, but then realized he couldn't possibly outfight them.

Another man stood towering before him, his long brown hair flowing just past his shoulders. Brown eyes stared coldly into his own.

"Where are you from and what are you doing here?" the man demanded in the language of Decimus' boyhood.

Decimus' mind began to churn frantically. He had to keep them away from the cave and Chara. When he tried again to jerk loose, he was lifted slightly from his feet. Hanging suspended in the air, he felt like a limp rag doll. These men had incredible strength.

"Answer me, or I'll slay you where you stand."

"My name is Decimus. I'm here seeking news of my tribe."

The giant fixed him with a dubious glance. "And what tribe might that be?"

"I am Cantiaci," he told them and had the satisfaction of seeing their faces change. Only the giant remained unfazed.

"And where have you been that you need to seek news now of your tribe?" he wanted to know.

Decimus was hesitant to tell them anything. In the end, he

decided to tell them a partial truth. "I have recently arrived from Rome where I was a slave." He glanced to the hill behind him, hoping that Chara wouldn't come looking for him.

"My name is Cadwaladyr, from the Trinovante tribe." The giant nodded to his men. "Release him."

They flung Decimus down, but he managed to keep his balance and stay on his feet. His hands clenched at his side. Now was not the time to try to induce a battle. He was hopelessly outnumbered, if not by numbers then definitely by sheer strength.

Cadwaladyr stood, arms folded across his chest, obviously awaiting an explanation. He was an imposing figure in his warrior garb. The temperatures were below freezing, yet the man wore only a pair of llawdyr and a bryean vest. The wool was treated with vinegar, Decimus knew, in a way that supposedly rendered the material so strong it could repel even a sword. His arms were bare, yet he gave no sign of feeling the cold.

"I have returned to Britannia seeking news of my family," Decimus told them truthfully. "I was taken prisoner by Roman soldiers almost twelve years ago. The last sight I had of my family was my father lying in a pool of blood, my mother across his chest, and my sister. . .my sister being passed from one Roman soldier to another."

Something flashed briefly in Cadwaladyr's eyes, but it was hidden instantly. "What were their names?"

"My father was Lucid, my mother Gamina, my sister Eudemia."

"Eudemia!"

The startled exclamation from the man on his right brought both Decimus' and Cadwaladyr's eyes to him. One look from Cadwaladyr and the other man closed his lips tightly.

Decimus turned back to Cadwaladyr. "You know her?"

Cadwaladyr shrugged. "Perhaps. Many girls have that name. Come, we will take you back to our village. Perhaps Der-wydd can help you."

Before Decimus could decide on his next move, a piercing

scream rent the air. Shoving Cadwaladyr aside, Decimus hurriedly climbed the hill behind him. The other three men were close on his heels.

Scrambling over the top, Decimus flung himself through the entrance to the cave, coming up short when he saw two men standing on each side of his wife. Before he could react, he was grabbed roughly from behind, finding himself once again a prisoner.

Cadwaladyr moved past him into the cave. He went quickly to Chara's side, jerking the sagum from her head.

Gritting his teeth, Decimus continued to struggle against the men who held him fast. "Leave her alone!"

Cadwaladyr studied Chara for a moment. Suddenly he smiled. "Many pardons, my lady. I thought you were someone else." He turned to Decimus, one dark brow arching. "We heard that there was a woman and her son living in a cave somewhere in the vicinity. We thought perhaps she was the one."

"She's my wife!"

Blinking, Cadwaladyr finally nodded to his men. They released him, and Decimus went quickly to Chara, taking her in his arms. He could feel her trembling as he whispered in Latin what Cadwaladyr had said.

"I know," she said softly. "This language is very similar to that which I grew up speaking in Gaul. I can't catch everything—but enough to be afraid."

Meanwhile, Cadwaladyr was studying the cave and its contents. Apparently, he was satisfied with what he saw.

"You stayed here to avoid the storm?"

Decimus nodded.

"Wise move. But our village will be safer. Gather your things and come with us."

Although the words were gently said, Decimus had no doubt that an order was behind them. The five men waited while they gathered their things. Decimus put out the fire, but left the wood. Perhaps Galla was on his way back even now. How could Decimus let him know what had happened?

"We need to hurry, Cadwaladyr. The storm is almost upon us."

Cadwaladyr was watching Decimus. "Bring their horses round."

Chara stayed close to her husband, her heart thudding with fear. What was to become of them now? And where, oh where, was Galla?

≈

Galla watched Eudemia as she worked around the cave. She was an industrious woman, her hands never idle for a moment.

Two days had gone by since he had entered their world. His head no longer pounded as it had, but a scab had formed on the laceration across his temple. The sore itself throbbed continually.

Eudemia had decided that he was not a threat, so she had released him. The only problem was that the winter storm had hit with a vengeance. He could not go out in the elements or he would be lost within minutes and dead a short time later.

The wind howled angrily outside their shelter. Galla felt the same violence roiling within himself. He was almost mad with worry over Decimus and Chara.

Had they stayed at the cave even after he hadn't returned in the appointed time? They had enough provisions. Hopefully Decimus had thought to bring the horses inside.

Cadvan sat silently in a corner, sharpening his knife with a stone. Periodically, he would look up and catch Galla's eyes on him. Frowning, he would turn himself slightly away.

"Is there anything I can do?" Galla questioned.

Eudemia looked at him in surprise. She thought for a moment, before shaking her head. "Not that I can think of."

"Perhaps he would like to help me fix the feathers to my arrows," Cadvan suggested.

Galla smiled at the boy. "I can do that."

Cadvan brought the feathers and long sticks that he had already prepared. He laid several sharpened stones next to them. They were well done, but Galla lifted curious eyes to his. "You have no iron or bronze?"

Without looking up, the boy answered him. "No."

Shrugging, Galla began to affix the feathers with swift, deft movements. The boy watched him, his eyes growing wide. Still, he said nothing.

Galla began to tell him stories, not of Rome and her conquests, but from Scriptures. Cadvan sat listening, enthralled.

Before long Eudemia joined them, a ball of yarn in her hands. She began twisting the yarn into lengths, the whole time listening intently to everything he said.

She looked up at one point. "The Druids have a story similar to the one you just told. What did you call the man?"

"Noah," Galla answered.

She nodded her head. "Much of what you have said, the Druids say also."

"Probably," Galla agreed. "Since God created the whole earth and everything in it, people are bound to have similar stories. Although the people wandered to different places on the earth after the tower of Babel, they still had the same beginnings."

She stared into Galla's eyes, and for the first time Galla noticed a softness there. "Funny how people can get things so turned around."

"Tell me of the Roman gods," Cadvan demanded. "Especially Mars."

Eudemia rose swiftly to her feet. "Enough. Enough about gods and their capriciousness. Go to the other cavern and bring back some wine."

Her son looked disappointed, but he obeyed. Galla watched him go, then turned to his mother. "You have a fine son."

She smiled. "Thank you. I think so."

"But there is one thing I must correct you on." She waited for him to continue. "My God is not capricious. He is unchanging, and His love is eternal."

She hesitated as though she wished to say something, but then she turned away. Galla watched her go back to her loom and begin weaving the threads in and out.

Cadvan came back with the wine. He placed the amphora on the table and then came back to help Galla with the arrows.

"You do this well," Galla told him. "Did your father teach you?"

The sudden silence in the room made Galla look up. Eudemia was frozen as though she were a statue. The boy looked from his mother back to Galla. "No. My father died before I was born."

"I'm sorry." Feeling uncomfortable, Galla hurried to change the subject. "How long have you lived here?"

Again Galla got the impression he was treading on thin ice. Not knowing what to say, he lapsed into silence.

"We've lived here since before Cadvan was born," Eudemia finally told him.

Galla decided retreat was in order. Leaning forward, he showed the boy how to better affix the arrows to give them more buoyancy. Cadvan smiled his appreciation.

The storm continued for three days. Cadvan seemed to follow Galla's every move. He was there whenever Galla returned from outside, he was there when Galla explored the cave, he was there when Galla helped prepare the meals.

Eudemia didn't miss the fact that her son had become enamored with the Roman. She smiled ruefully. No matter how hard she tried, some things only a man could provide.

"The snow is beginning to lessen," Galla told them, watching the swirling layers of whiteness. Dropping the fur curtain, he turned back to the room.

Eudemia nodded. "It should stop by tomorrow."

For some reason, Galla felt reluctant to leave, but he knew he must. Almost a week had passed since he had left Chara and Decimus.

That evening when they sat down to their meal, Galla told them about his two friends. Eudemia was surprised. "What did you say his name was?"

"Decimus."

She looked down, her lip beginning to tremble. He saw

such pain in her eyes that Galla felt moved to comfort her.

"What is it?" he whispered.

She shook her head slightly. "I had a younger brother by that name."

"What happened to him?"

Suddenly she looked up, glaring into his eyes. "The Romans took him. I doubt he's still alive. Most likely he was sent to the galleys."

Galla felt the color leave his face. Could it be possible? Could Eudemia's brother and Decimus be one and the same? The resemblance was there, and hadn't Decimus mentioned the name *Eudemia?* What a streak of fate that would be. But stay. Fate? There was no such thing. Had God arranged this all along? And if so, what else had He planned?

Galla bit his lip in indecision. Should he tell Eudemia his suspicions, or would that get her hopes up too high? Finally, he decided to confide in her.

That night when they lay down, Galla knew he would never get to sleep. He lay staring up at the flickering shadows caused by the fire from the brazier.

"Galla?"

Galla turned toward the soft voice. Eudemia rose from her mat and came to sit next to him. She looked down, her hair falling forward to conceal her cheeks. She looked so much like Chara in one of her shy moods that Galla almost reached out to touch her.

"There is something I need to tell you," she told him softly, glancing at her son to make sure he was asleep. His even breathing told her it was safe to continue.

Looking back at the ground, she started to talk to him, so softly he had to strain to hear her. Finally, he moved closer, watching her face in the semidarkness.

"Twelve years ago, Romans attacked our village. They killed my mother and father, took away my brother, and. . ." She stopped. When she continued, he heard tears in her voice. "The soldiers, they. . .they. . ."

Suddenly Galla understood. He took her hand into his. Hers was like ice. "I understand."

Nodding, she continued. "I became pregnant. When my tribesmen found out they decided. . .the Druids thought my child would make a perfect sacrifice."

Galla's eyes went wide. It was true then. The Druids did offer human sacrifices.

Eudemia looked into his face, her eyes burning intensely. "He may not have been born of love, but he is a part of me. I told them no." She grimaced. "Cadwaladyr wanted me for his wife, but he refused to have a Roman brat for a son. He plotted with the Druids. My best friend, Brianna, heard them talking and came to tell me." She gripped his hand tightly as she continued to remember. "I ran away. Cadwaladyr tracked me, but winter was setting in. Miraculously, I found this cave. It's so well hidden that it's hard to spot unless you are right up on it. Cadwaladyr had to return to the village because heavy snows came. This part of Britannia usually has mild winters, but for the last twelve years the winters have been hard and cold. Another miracle, for it has made it harder for us to be found."

Privately, Galla agreed that God's hand had been miraculously on Eudemia's life.

"Cadwaladyr has never stopped looking for me. I'm not sure why." Galla could have told her. "But anyway, he's never been able to find me. Once or twice when I was away hunting, he has almost caught up with me. But each time I was able to evade him and get back to this cave safely."

She looked at him again. "You asked Cadvan who taught him to set arrows. I did."

Galla was surprised. "And who taught you?"

She was quiet a long time. "Decimus."

❧

When Decimus and Chara rode into the village, several people hurried out to meet them. Men, women, and children stood gawking at the visitors. One young boy ran to the other end of the village.

Chara was captivated by the dwellings. They were round, and instead of tiles on the roofs, these were thatched.

The young boy returned, followed by an elderly man in white robes. Decimus felt the tension coil tightly within him. The man was a priest, and from the look of him, the druid high priest, or archdruid as they called him.

His white robes flowed around him, cinched at the waist by a girdle of gold encasing a blue crystal. A gold tiara rested on his white locks and round his forehead he wore the sacred mistletoe.

Decimus remembered now. The ring on the old man's hand was the chain ring of divination. Around his neck was the Jodhain Morain, or breastplate of judgment. Supposedly it had the power to squeeze the neck of anyone uttering a false judgment. Since Decimus doubted that was true, he certainly hoped he wasn't called upon to challenge the man's word.

"Der-wydd, we have visitors." Cadwaladyr dismounted, handing the reins of his horse to one of his men.

The druid looked from Decimus to Chara and back to Decimus. There seemed to be a flicker of recognition in his eyes, but he waited for an explanation.

Cadwaladyr moved closer to the priest, with his hand indicating Decimus. "The man claims to be of your tribe. He has come searching for news of his family."

The druid glanced sideways at Cadwaladyr, but immediately turned his attention back to Decimus. "I see. What is your family?"

"His sister's name is Eudemia." Cadwaladyr frowned at the young man who spoke.

"Indeed. And your father and mother?"

"My father's name was Lucid. My mother Gamina." Decimus felt a deep pain in his chest as he accepted at last what he had always suspected. "I think they are both dead."

Sucking in a breath, the druid motioned for everyone to step aside. Nodding his head at Cadwaladyr, the druid indicated that Decimus and Chara were to follow him.

Decimus felt Cadwaladyr close on his heels as though to prevent any chance of escape. The hair prickled on the nape of his neck. He felt more trapped than he had sitting in that warehouse in Rome. The druid stopped beside one of the larger houses in the village. Motioning them inside, he followed and closed the door.

The main room had little furniture. Cubicles in the plaster walls held numerous scrolls. A brazier was lit, giving light to the semidark room.

The druid seated himself on one of the couches, indicating that Decimus and Chara should sit across from him. When they were seated, Decimus became aware that Cadwaladyr was still in the room. He could feel the man's eyes on his back.

"We know of your family," the old druid stated.

Excitement gleamed in Decimus' eyes as he leaned forward. "Are they still alive?"

The old man shook his head, his eyes grave. "Lucid and Gamina were killed by the Romans. As we feared you had been." His face softened. "I remember you from your youth," he told Decimus. "You were impatient and headstrong even then."

Decimus tried to remember, but he seemed to have a mental block. No picture would come. The regalia he could remember, the man he could not. He shut his eyes for a moment, letting his acceptance of his parents' deaths wash over him.

The druid looked at Cadwaladyr. "Perhaps you remember Cadwaladyr?"

Decimus turned back to the other man, studying him with narrowed eyes. Slowly, he shook his head. "Should I?"

"Well, perhaps not," the druid answered. "It was a long time ago, and you were but a boy. Cadwaladyr and others from his tribe fought with us against the Romans—but our forces were not enough."

"And my sister? What of Eudemia?"

Cadwaladyr stepped forward. "She is alive."

Decimus came to his feet. "Where is she?"

Shaking his head, the old druid shrugged his shoulders. "We don't know. After she became pregnant, she ran off into the hills to hide. No one could find her."

Sinking back to the couch, Decimus was barely aware of Chara taking his hand. "Then she's probably dead. No woman could survive out there alone. Especially if she was with child."

"She is alive," Cadwaladyr insisted. "We haven't been able to find her, but we have found evidence over the years of places she has been."

Decimus stared at the man, his mind beginning to question the man's integrity. "You make it sound as if she doesn't want to be found."

"She doesn't."

Decimus looked from Cadwaladyr to the old druid. "What's going on here? You're not telling me something."

The two exchanged glances. Finally the old man sighed. "You are right. There is more, but you won't like it."

The druid told Decimus how at the time these things had happened, he had been far away attending a judgment in another village. He explained to Decimus how the other druids had planned to sacrifice Eudemia's child to the gods, hoping to gain support in their fight against the Romans since the child was part Roman.

Chara listened carefully, growing accustomed to the strange dialect and accent. She was appalled at their callousness regarding a child. A baby at that. Unconsciously, her hand went to her stomach. Decimus was right. This was no place to raise a child.

Decimus glared at Cadwaladyr, his hands clenching and un-clenching at his side. The man's veiled eyes stared impassively back at him.

"I'm not proud of my part in this," he told Decimus. "Der-wydd told us that the gods would judge us harshly for our acts. He made us see our error. I have tried to make amends, but I have not been able to find her."

Decimus remembered the times he had gone with his sister out into the hills, while their father taught them to hunt and track. Their father had been the finest tracker in all of the countryside, and he had taught Decimus and his sister well. No wonder they had never been able to find her. If she chose not to be found, he had no doubt that they wouldn't find her.

"You've tried to find her for twelve years?"

Surprisingly, Cadwaladyr blushed. "Your sister is a remarkable woman."

"Aye, she is that," the old druid agreed. "Perhaps you can join us in helping to track her down. Then we can lay all of this to rest once and for all."

Rising to his feet, Der-wydd smiled at Chara. "You must have a place to stay." Turning back to Decimus, he touched him on the shoulder. "Your father's house still stands. We have cared for it, just in case your sister did return to us some day. Cadwaladyr will show you the way."

When Decimus stepped across the threshold of his old house, memories came swarming back to greet him. Everything was much as he remembered, except he could tell several repairs had been made to the house. Cadwaladyr told Decimus how they had found the house partially burned by the Romans when they returned that fateful day.

"I'll leave you now. Someone from the village will bring you food."

Decimus watched him go, wondering if he had made a mistake in trusting these people. Chara came up and slid an arm around his waist. He smiled down at her.

"So much has happened," she told him softly.

"My mind is in total confusion," he agreed. "Somewhere out there is my sister. I wonder if her child lived?"

Chara stared pensively at the surrounding hills. Darkness was beginning to fall and winter had set in with a surety. "I don't know, but out there somewhere is Galla, also. I pray to God he's all right and that he will be able to find us."

thirteen

Cadvan looked up from the floor of the cave where he was kneeling. The light from the entrance showed clearly the tension on his face.

"There were five men, one smaller than the others, and a woman." His hand stroked one of the footprints. "This man is very large."

Eudemia blew out her breath in a sigh. "Cadwaladyr."

The boy nodded. "I believe so."

Alarmed, Galla began to search the cave. There had been no evidence of anything untoward from the outside, but the snow had covered everything to a depth of several inches.

"You won't find them here," Cadvan told him. Galla looked at the boy, once more aware of how old he seemed for his age.

"How do you know?"

"There was a struggle. Here." He pointed to a spot on the floor and Galla noticed what he had missed before. The dirt was disturbed in a violent manner, obviously from a scuffle.

"All the footprints lead out," Eudemia agreed. "Whatever happened, they seem to have gone willingly."

Galla stared helplessly around. No tracks were left outside to follow. What was he to do now?

"They are probably traveling to the village," Cadvan suggested.

Galla's face seemed etched in granite, his eyes becoming the color of iron in their intensity. "Then that's where I must go."

Eudemia felt her heart drop. What did this one Roman think he could do against a whole tribe? He would be killed. Her eyes grew wide as she realized she didn't want to see this happen. She didn't even want him to leave.

Cadvan went to the entrance to the cave and studied the sky. "I think that will have to wait," he told Galla.

Galla was already shaking his head. "I haven't time to lose. I have to try and help my friends."

Shrugging, Cadvan turned back to the cave. "It will be hard to help them if you are dead."

"Cadvan!"

"It's true, Mother. Another storm is about to hit. It doesn't look as though it will be as strong as the first, but it will still be a killer for anyone unfortunate enough to be stuck out in it." He looked at Galla. "We have barely enough time to get back to our own cave."

"How far to the village?" Galla wanted to know, still unconvinced.

Eudemia answered him. "About half a day's ride north."

Galla continued to study the terrain outside the cave. The other two waited for his answer. Galla's first instinct was to try for the village, but he realized that would be foolish. Sighing, he glanced at the others. "Let's go back to your cave. As soon as the storm passes, I will set out to find them."

When the snow began, it fell lightly at first, but it rapidly turned into a full blizzard. Galla shook his head. This was not the weather his father had described when he had told him of Britannia. Galla had always heard that the winters were mild, the summers cool, but the snow that fell now was as cold and heavy as that which he'd seen high in the mountains north of Rome. He began to fret at his enforced inactivity. He should be trying to find Decimus and Chara.

Five men and one woman. Cadvan's words kept coming back to haunt him. One woman alone with all of those men. Galla swallowed the knot that formed in his throat. His eyes took on a feral gleam. If anything happened to Chara *or* Decimus. . .He shook his head to free himself of such thinking. Where had such murderous thoughts come from? Decimus and Chara were in God's hands, just as they had been all along.

He jumped when Eudemia laid a hand on his arm. "Your thoughts are far from pleasant. You are worried about your friends?"

It was more a statement than a question. Nodding his head, he smiled slightly. "You are right, my thoughts *were* far from pleasant. I'm afraid they were far from *Christ-like* also."

"Your God doesn't approve of killing?"

Galla thought before answering. "My God doesn't approve of *murder*."

Eudemia frowned. "Is there a difference?"

Sighing, Galla sat down on his pallet. "I think so. The Scriptures tell us that David was a man after God's own heart, yet he killed hundreds of men and was responsible for thousands of other deaths."

"Even women and children?"

"I'm afraid so."

Glaring, Eudemia threw herself down beside him. "This doesn't make sense. Why make war on children?"

Galla stared intently into her icy blue eyes. "Why offer them as sacrifices? Why make them slaves? Why leave them on the rocks to die?"

With each question, Eudemia watched Galla's face become more and more savage. He had a heart for children, this one. He would make a fine father. Sensing his reluctance to discuss the subject, still she pressed on. She had to know.

"So it is all right for soldiers to kill?"

Instead of answering her question, Galla began to tell her a story. "Several years ago, my father met a man who had been to see Jesus' cousin. The cousin's name was John, but everyone called him "the Baptizer." This soldier asked John what he had to do to be in accord with God's will."

Curious, Eudemia's eyes roved over Galla's solemn features. "And he told him not to kill?"

Galla shook his head. "No. He told him not to extort money from the people or accuse people falsely, to be content with his pay."

"But to make war on children!"

"War is bad anytime," he told her. "But sometimes it is necessary."

Unexpectedly, Galla smiled as he watched Eudemia's animated features. She was so passionate about everything! Her heart was so full of love and gentleness, and she cared about life. All life. She hadn't even held it against him that he was a despised Roman.

She was so hungry for God's peace, yet she didn't even realize she was. Galla tried to explain again about God's gift of salvation. He could tell that she didn't understand, but she wanted to. She continued asking him questions long into the night.

Cadvan had stopped listening to them long ago. His deep, even breathing told them that he was fast asleep. Eudemia rose and went to him, pulling the furs securely around him. Her love flowed out of her eyes as she stroked the boy's cheek.

Galla felt a lump in his own throat as he watched her. She had so much love to give. How could her people have treated her so cruelly?

She came back and sat down across from him again. She looked him in the eye and suddenly, to Galla, the cave seemed terribly warm. Before, her eyes had been icy blue. Now they were the warm tranquil blue of the Mediterranean. He felt himself hypnotized by their iridescence, the lights flickering in their depths.

"Tell me more of your God," she demanded softly, and Galla did so, unaware of what he was really saying. The words came, but his thoughts were not with them. His thoughts were focused on the pair of soft lips smiling so closely to his own. He had only to move a fraction. . .

"Galla."

Her soft entreaty sent a warm fire racing through him. He tried to keep his self-control, but it was a lost cause. Leaning forward, he closed the distance between them.

She responded to his kiss with a fervor that surprised him. As her arms wound their way around his neck, he felt his defenses beginning to crumble. Pulling her to him, he intensified their kiss.

Keep yourself pure. Where had the thought come from?

Galla felt his ardor beginning to cool. Pulling away slightly, he stared down into Eudemia's face. She watched him, puzzled at his resistance.

Galla pushed her gently away. "Go to bed, Eudemia." His voice was harsh to his own ears. God had once again saved him from his own weak nature.

Miffed, Eudemia rose quickly to her feet. Without looking at him, she went to her pallet and lay down.

Galla stared up at the ceiling. He had every nook and cranny memorized by now, knew where every shadow was, every hole. He sighed. This was going to be a long night.

❧

Chara smiled at the woman standing before her. Although she was not beautiful, her features were pleasant. Her soft, blue eyes held a softness that spoke of a gentleness within.

"Tell me, Brianna, what is everyone doing?"

The young woman smiled back at her. "We are getting ready for Samhain. The boys will climb the oak trees to find mistletoe, while the girls will weave it into headpieces. Everyone will gather oak, our sacred wood, to be burned in a huge bonfire. You will see. We must each find a rock, also."

The smile fled from Chara's face. Samhain? Was this some kind of pagan rite?

"What is the purpose of the rocks?" she wanted to know.

Brianna continued to empty her baskets of their contents. For days now the people of the village had supplied them with food. Although Decimus could pay for the goods, he was as yet unwilling to do so. He told her that he wasn't sure these people would have much use for coins, so instead Chara traded with them.

"Everyone will write their names on a rock and then later throw them into the bonfire. If the rocks are still there in the morning, all is well. If your rock is gone. . ."

"Yes?"

"If the rock with your name on it is gone, then you will die sometime in the coming year."

Chara shivered at her casual reference to death. She watched the woman gather her things together in preparation for leaving. She couldn't be so very old, yet there was a sadness about her that never seemed to go away.

Was it the fact that she was in love with Cadwaladyr, but he didn't return that love? The man barely registered Brianna's existence. But that didn't stop Brianna from following the giant with her eyes, her love shining through.

Impulsively, Chara laid a hand on the girl's arm. "Brianna, have you ever heard of Jesus Christ?"

She shook her head, smiling into Chara's face. Chara wanted to seize the moment and speak of Christ to the woman, but something held her back.

"Never mind," she finally told her and watched as the other girl left the house. Chara went to the window and saw Brianna heading down the hill in the direction of the village, picking up loose oak branches she found along the way.

Chara shook her head. This place was so far from Rome, yet its religion was much the same. Only Romans didn't offer human sacrifices to their gods, except for the gladiators, of course. She saw Brianna stop to talk with Decimus as he rounded the bend and came into sight. He laughed at something she said, and Chara felt the first stirrings of jealousy. These were his people, she was an outsider.

Decimus came in the door, laying his mantle across a stool. He briskly rubbed his hands together before the fire. "Cadwaladyr says that after tomorrow we can go search for Galla."

"Why after tomorrow?"

"No one will travel tomorrow. It's a feast day. Everyone will be celebrating, or feeling the effects thereof."

Chara placed a bowl of stew on the table for him, its steam curling invitingly into the air. "Sit down and eat." Seating herself across from him, she frowned at him. "Brianna was telling me something about this Samhain celebration."

Decimus began hungrily devouring the food. In between

bites he managed to tell her more of their superstitious beliefs.

"So they believe this Samhain, this god of the dead, allows the souls of the dead to return for this one night?"

He nodded. "Before the end of the day, Der-wydd will come and tell us to put out our fire. Then we will relight it from the bonfire they will build."

Chara rose from her seat, taking the empty bowls from the table. "And what of the sacrifices?"

Decimus brow furrowed in thought. "I'm not sure there will be any. I don't understand this festival myself."

"And will we be required to participate in it?"

Decimus' frown deepened. "Of course not. Their gods are not our God. Why ask such a thing?"

Chara shrugged. "Just the way Brianna spoke. She seemed to assume we would be a part of the celebration."

Sighing heavily, Decimus got up from his seat and took Chara into his arms. "Let's worry about that when the time comes."

She clung to him, closing her eyes. "Oh, Decimus, these people are so. . .so *pagan*."

"So were we at one time," he told her. Chara shook her head, and Decimus remembered that she had been raised as a Christian. He smiled. "Sometimes I forget how pure you are."

She flushed with color. Decimus found her enchanting, a mixture of innocence and desire. Even now her eyes spoke clearly to him. Before he could take advantage of the situation, a pounding shook his door.

Opening the portal, Decimus found himself face to face with Der-wydd. "It is time to put out your hearth fire and come to the ceremony of the Samhain."

Decimus hesitated. Did watching the ceremony mean he was participating in it? He thought not and he wanted to understand these people. How could he ever hope to reach them otherwise?

They followed Der-wydd as he headed back down the hill to the village, his long white robes taking on the colors of the sunset. The evening sun reflected brightly off his golden tiara. For a man his age, he was still spry.

Decimus and Chara continued to the village, while Der-wydd continued on his journey to the other villagers. Already a huge pile of wood was gathered at the end of the village. Many were already in the midst of celebrating the coming of a new year. Strong beer, the favored drink of these people, was flowing freely from person to person.

Chara shrunk closer to Decimus' side. These festivities reminded her of the stories her mother had told her of Moses, when the people had built the golden calf as he was talking to God on the mountain.

A young girl screamed as she was lifted over the shoulder of a burly young man. Grinning, he spun her around and around, finally falling in a heap in the soft snow. Bodies entwined, they laughed uproariously.

Frowning down at his wife, Decimus took her hand safely and securely within his own. Maybe coming to the celebration hadn't been a good idea after all.

Darkness descended, but the revelry continued. Cheers went up from the gathered crowd as Der-wydd lit the now huge stack of wood. Louder and louder rose the voices of the people. Soon, Decimus realized that they were chanting, their bodies swaying back and forth. Their movements and their sing-song voices soon had him in a semihypnotized state. Shaking his head to free himself of the effects, he glanced down at Chara to see how she was affected. Her eyes were closed and her lips were moving.

Grinning, he felt a curious pride that nothing seemed to affect her relationship with her God. Come what may, she would hold her own.

The fire was beginning to die down, yet was still bright enough to allow a bright halo of light far down the streets of the village. Some of the older people were making their way to their houses, torches from the bonfire lighting their way. Only the youngest remained, and most of them were so drunk on the strong brew they craved, Decimus doubted they could see to find their way home. As people left, they threw their rocks into the fire, hoping that they would still be there come morning.

Cadwaladyr was making his way toward them, only slightly staggering. As he reached them, he held out his hands. In the curve of each palm rested a rock, one with Chara's name and the other with Decimus'.

Chara frowned, not realizing that the rock was meant for her. *Strange*, Decimus thought, *that I can still recognize my name written in the Celtic language.*

Cadwaladyr bowed low before Chara, stumbling slightly. Decimus sucked in his breath, moving to place himself between them. If the big giant were to fall on Chara, he would surely crush the life from her.

"For you, my lady."

Chara slowly reached out a hand. Looking up into Cadwaladyr's face, she realized that this was a test. Since the rock held no symbolic significance for her, she turned and threw it into the fire. When she turned back to Cadwaladyr, his eyebrows were raised slightly.

"May the gods not choose your rock," he told her.

Decimus hid a grin behind his fingers. Cadwaladyr looked as though he were disappointed. Had he hoped that they would defy the gods?

A disturbance at the other end of the fire brought their attention elsewhere. A young man was close to the fire, swaying back and forth. In his hands he held a small squirrel, swinging it over his head. In his other he held a gleaming knife. In one quick movement he slit the squirrel's throat.

Chara gasped, burying her head in Decimus' arm. Decimus watched in fascination as the boy drained the blood from the animal and then threw in into the fire. Cheers rose from the onlookers as they spurred him on. Again they took up their chant, their bodies swaying to the rhythm.

Decimus put his arm around his wife and turned to Cadwaladyr. "My wife has had enough. I'll take her home now."

Cadwaladyr grinned, aware of their real reason for leaving. "Aren't you going to stay for the reading of the bones? I will be throwing in my own sacrifice so that Der-wydd can tell me my destiny."

Before Decimus could answer, a woman's voice spoke eerily from the darkness beyond the fire. "You needn't wait for the readings, Cadwaladyr. *I* can tell you your destiny."

An uncanny silence descended on the whole group. Squinting his eyes to see better, Cadwaladyr strained to see the owner of the voice. A shadow moved from the darkness and into the light. Cadwaladyr gasped as the woman became visible.

"Eudemia!"

fourteen

Galla stared over Eudemia's head at the giant standing before the roaring fire. Although Galla knew he himself was big, standing at least six feet, this man would tower over him by at least six more inches.

Never had he seen a man sober up as fast as this one did. His eyes never left Eudemia, as though he believed himself to be hallucinating. For a moment Eudemia returned his stare, her own eyes challenging, before she looked to his side.

Decimus stood beside the giant, his look of wonder telling Galla better than words could have that Decimus recognized his sister. They stood contemplating each other several moments before Eudemia let out a cry, running into her brother's arms.

Galla's searching gaze found Chara, puzzled and uncertain beside her husband. In all the time they had known Decimus, he had rarely shown any emotion. Now his face was wet with his tears.

Chara spotted Galla and was instantly running across the darkness, throwing herself at him. "You're alive! Thank God, you're alive!"

Squeezing her tightly, Galla felt his own eyes brimming with tears. "I thought I would never see you two again."

Looking over her shoulder, Galla's eyes met Decimus'. They smiled at each other, and Galla pulled Chara with him to their side.

Forgetting everything, they laughed and hugged, content to be together again. A shadow looming over them brought them to sudden silence.

Cadwaladyr stood towering over them, his dark eyes unblinking. Slowly his gaze roved over Eudemia. Instead of cringing away, she pulled herself to her full height, which, compared to Chara's, was considerable.

"So tell me my destiny," he growled.

Shaking her head, she glared up at him. "There will be only one destiny for you if you continue to hunt me and my son. Several times we could have struck you dead, yet we did not. But I have had enough now."

She pulled a leather girdle from inside her sagum and handed it to the big man. His eyes went wide.

"Where did you get this?"

"I took it from your horse last spring when you camped near my home."

His admiring look didn't please Galla at all. There were things here he didn't understand but he was determined to find out about them.

Most of the crowd of people had dispersed at Eudemia's sudden appearance, their eyes filled with terror. He didn't know that according to their supersitions the dead were supposed to walk the earth this night. Nor could he know that they believed Eudemia to have been one of those freed by Samhain, their god of the dead.

Decimus spoke up. "Let's go to Der-wydd. He must know that Eudemia has returned."

Cadwaladyr nodded once, his eyes never leaving Eudemia's face. Galla felt himself beginning to bristle at the man's constant attention.

Der-wydd explained the story to Eudemia the same way he had explained it Decimus. There was a kindness in the old man that caused Decimus to doubt his involvement with the happenings of that time so many years ago.

But if he was not a part of it, where were the other druids who were? There had been no sign of other druids in the vicinity, not even a young bard in training.

Decimus learned that he had a nephew. They decided that Cadwaladyr, Galla, and Eudemia would leave at first light to fetch Cadvan. An undercurrent of tension flowed between the big man and Eudemia, as though they still had unfinished business between them.

For now, Decimus felt at peace. He had found his people and was reunited with his sister. Soon his nephew would join them and they would be a family. Life was good. God was good.

❧

When Cadvan joined them, he soon fit in with the community. The other boys were impressed with his hunting and tracking skills. He shared with them the new way Galla had showed him to affix feathers to their arrows, and they made sport seeing whose arrows could go the farthest.

One day, Chara was returning from the village when she spotted Eudemia and Cadwaladyr arguing on the path. Neither noticed her and she stopped, afraid to go on. So heated was their argument, Chara had no trouble hearing what was being said.

"You were promised to me long ago, Eudemia. You belong to me."

Shoving a forefinger into the big man's chest, Eudemia punctuated her words with sharp, angry thrusts. "Never will I belong to you! You would have killed my son! Given half a chance, you would have killed me for defying you."

"That's not true," he argued. "That's why I left my people, my home, to come and wed you."

"Bah! Your thirst for blood brought you here. You wanted to kill *Romans!*"

Chara shoved her hands hard against her ears, yet still their voices reached her clearly.

"It's that Roman you came back with, isn't it? You prefer a Roman dog to me, one of your own people."

Eudemia's eyes glowed like blue ice as she stared angrily into Cadwaladyr's. Turning, she strode away from the big man, heading for the house. He caught up with her in two strides. Gripping her by the arms, he pulled her forcefully against his chest.

"You will be my wife, or no one's. I have the right, and if necessary, I will challenge the Roman to a fight."

Eudemia's face paled. "He would not fight you. He does not want me."

Cadwaladyr threw back his head, his brown eyes gleaming like polished bronze. "He wants you, all right. I see how he looks at you." Shoving her away, he turned on his heels. "Remember what I said."

He stopped when he reached Chara's side, his eyes narrowing. "You have something to say, woman?"

Chara watched him silently, her eyes never leaving his. He was the one who first looked away. Without saying anything, Chara followed Eudemia to the house.

After that, Chara noticed Cadwaladyr watching Eudemia whenever he was near. Wherever she happened to be, he was there also. Eudemia ignored him although Chara knew she was aware of him.

Chara shared her concerns with Decimus, telling him about the conversation she overheard. After much consideration, she decided not to tell him about Cadwaladyr's threat to Galla.

Decimus started watching his sister more carefully. Whatever Cadwaladyr's plans, Decimus had no doubt that Eudemia could handle the man; however, he wanted to head off any trouble before it occurred.

Although Decimus and Eudemia had assured Galla that there was plenty of room in their home, he had chosen to build himself a small one of his own closer to the village. Chara thought it might have something to do with the fact that due to Cadvan's hero worship of the Roman, the other boys followed him also. She noticed that he took every opportunity to share stories of Jesus with them, and though they didn't show much interest, neither did they turn away.

For the first time in weeks, Galla had joined them for the

evening meal. He smiled as Eudemia laid his plate on the table in front of him. She in turn blushed a rosy red.

Decimus was not unaware of his sister's attraction to Galla. He watched them to see if there was any sign of a returned affection. Although he loved the Roman, he loved his sister more and he didn't wish to see her hurt.

Galla pulled the meat from the bones of the quail he was eating, dipping it in the broth. Decimus sensed he had something on his mind.

"I'll be leaving in a few days to go north to Trinovante country."

Slowly he looked up, finding four pair of eyes riveted to his face.

"It's time for me to find my own people and fulfill my duties."

"You aren't really going to try to turn the Trinovante against the other tribes," Decimus argued.

"That is not my intention," Galla returned quietly. "You have found your family, now I have a yearning to see my own." Although that was partly true, Galla hid his real reason for leaving.

"But Galla," Cadvan wailed. "You said you would teach me to fight like the Romans."

Eudemia said nothing. Suddenly her appetite was gone. Had Cadwaladyr threatened Galla? Was he fleeing because he was a coward? Or did he realize how she felt about him and he wanted to get as far away as possible?

"We'll miss you," Chara told him softly, and Galla returned her smile.

"As I will you. All of you," he told them, his eyes fixing on Eudemia.

Cadvan flung himself away from the table, running to the ladder that led to the house's loft. They could hear his sobs through the ceiling. Galla swallowed hard, rising to his feet. He started to go to the boy, but stopped himself. It was better this way. Gritting his teeth, he turned to the others.

"I have to leave now." Without looking at them, he gathered his sagum and his bow that he carried with him. "I'll talk to you tomorrow."

After he left, Eudemia hurriedly rose to her feet. "I'll get some wood for the fire."

Both Chara and Decimus refrained from comment on the full stack of wood in the corner.

Eudemia hurried after Galla, calling him urgently. He turned when he heard her voice, waiting for her to reach him. She stopped in front of him, her eyes liquid in the moonlight.

"You have to leave?" she asked him, biting her lip to keep it from trembling.

Galla heaved a sigh, reaching out a hand to stroke down her cheek. "Yes."

"Why?"

Frowning, he turned to study the trees that grew beside the path. "I told you why. I have an assignment to fulfill."

"And will you return?"

He was so quiet, Eudemia thought he wasn't going to answer. "Galla?"

"I don't know. I have no reason to. Decimus can do here what needs to be done, and I can go elsewhere. Together, we can cover more territory with the Word."

She shook her head angrily. "I don't know what you're talking about, I only know I want you to stay."

Galla's insides twisted at the tears in her voice. He didn't want to hurt her, but he couldn't stay. He didn't trust himself. She was a nonbeliever, and as such, he couldn't contemplate a future with her.

He closed his eyes. On the other hand, he couldn't contemplate a future without her, either. He had finally admitted to himself that he loved her. And Cadvan. The boy was so eager, so bright. So easy to love.

Determined to make him see, Eudemia put her arms

around his neck, pulling his head down to hers. She kissed him fully on the lips. Galla could taste the salt from her tears.

Throwing pride to the wind, she begged him softly, "Please stay. Please don't go. I love you."

Her words immediately filled him with joy, but just as quickly the pain followed. He wasn't pretending when he said he had an job to finish. He had sworn to serve Rome's army, and he would keep his vow. He had sworn to serve his God, and he would keep that promise also.

Taking her hands from his neck, he folded them in front of her. His eyes watched her intently. "I have to go."

"It's Cadwaladyr, isn't it? He's frightened you away!"

Galla frowned. "What are you talking about? Cadwaladyr has nothing to do with this."

She continued to cry. "No matter what you say, no matter what you do, I *won't* marry him."

Galla felt himself go cold inside. Gripping her arms, he shook her slightly. "What are you saying? Who said anything about marrying Cadwaladyr?"

Eudemia told him of the promise between her parents and Cadwaladyr's. A hope of uniting the two tribes with a marriage between two noble houses.

Releasing her, Galla shoved one hand back through his dark hair, glaring at the sky. The bright moon cast light over the terrain around them, causing everything to be highlighted by dark shadows.

Regardless of his feelings, he had to go. Nothing had changed. He still had a job to do, and Eudemia was still a nonbeliever.

Taking her face between his palms, Galla softly kissed her lips. "I love you, Eudemia. But I have to go. I can't marry you. There are reasons, but most of them you probably wouldn't understand."

Seeing the hope die in her eyes was almost more than he

could bear. Turning, he quickly retreated down the hill. Eudemia watched him go, tears coursing a path down her cheeks.

He had said he loved her and her heart flowed with joy. She would go to him tomorrow. No matter what his reasons, she would try again.

≈

The next day, Galla was gone. Eudemia had found the hut where he lived empty.

His absence affected nearly everyone. Decimus missed the Roman more than he thought possible. He had grown to love him like a brother and he missed his wise counsel. Chara cried for her friend, but more than that she prayed for him. Hopefully, he would be able to send them word wherever he went.

There was one person who missed Galla for a different reason. Brianna had hoped the Roman would marry Eudemia, and then in turn she hoped that Cadwaladyr would notice her.

Life went on in the village. The inhabitants came to realize that Chara and Decimus served a different God, but although they were curious, they didn't feel intimidated. They couldn't believe that anyone as loving and kind as Chara could be a threat to their lives.

Brianna brought bread to the house one day while Decimus and Eudemia were out hunting with Cadvan. Brianna exchanged bread for some of the salt Chara had brought with them. Today, Brianna didn't immediately rush off as she usually did. Instead, she began fiddling with Chara's sewing that was sitting on the table.

"Did you wish to speak with me, Brianna?" Chara asked her.

The other woman sat down at the table, twisting her hands in her lap. "I. . .I wanted to hear about this God you serve."

Joyfully, Chara told her all that she knew about God and she shared what she had been taught from the Apostles' writings.

Brianna sighed. "It would be nice to be loved like that. I

have noticed that you and Decimus aren't fearful like the rest of us. You don't fear the dark, or the storms, or even death."

Chara smiled wryly. "We're all afraid of something." She then told Brianna about her life, her trip through captivity, her marriage to Decimus.

Brianna's face was filled with awe. "Your God has truly taken care of you. Could He. . .could He love *me* that much, do you think?"

Taking her hand, Chara told her, "He already does."

Later, Chara watched Brianna walking down the path that led to the village. Whatever was on the girl's heart seemed to weigh down her steps.

That night Chara shared the happy news of Brianna's search for the one true God. Decimus smiled, his eyes roving her joyful countenance.

"I have seen fruit from some of the seeds we have planted, also. Illtud and some of the others are beginning to realize that their fears are what make them weak. I have told them that perfect love drives out fear." He grinned. "It's been several months, but already many of the people are beginning to question the old ways."

Feeling a sense of unease, Chara frowned. "What of Der-wydd? How will he take the proselytizing of his people?"

Decimus sat down on the couch, pulling her down with him. "You know, I think he doesn't mind. I'm not sure why, maybe it's an answer to prayer, but Der-wydd seems relieved that many of his people no longer request sacrifices to tell their futures or plan their lives."

"And what of Cadwaladyr?"

He shrugged. "Cadwaladyr has left the village. He has followed Galla back to the Trinovantes, though I'm not sure why."

Chara looked alarmed. "Will he try to hurt Galla?"

Decimus pressed his lips together. "I don't know, but I'm betting Galla can take care of himself. Remember, he has God on his side."

Bending his head, Decimus began to nibble on Chara's neck. Giggling, she pulled away. "Cadvan might come."

Decimus slowly shook his head, his blue eyes gleaming. "He is staying the night with a friend. They want to start early on a hunt."

As he bent to her again, she pushed him away. "Eudemia might come."

Again he slowly shook his head. "She plans to go with Cadvan in the morning, so she has decided to stay with Kolin's family, also." He raised an eyebrow. "Any more objections?"

Shaking her head, she grinned, nibbling his chin. "None, my love."

❧

Isolated as they were from the other tribes, news took weeks, sometimes months, to reach their village. One day, a rider rode in from the outside and informed them that Nero was dead. A ripple of voices could be heard from the gathered crowd. No one knew what this would mean for Britannia.

"How did he die?" Decimus asked, pulling Chara close to his side.

"Committed suicide," the rider told them. "His army turned against him."

"Who is in charge now?"

"General Galba. You know of him?" he asked Decimus.

Decimus nodded his head. "He's an old man, but I heard he was a wise general. God only knows how he'll be as Caesar."

On their way home, Chara commented softly to her husband, "It's hard to believe he's dead."

Decimus shook his head. "What a wasted life. I would not want to be Nero when he stands before God's throne."

Remembering Agrippina and Antipus, Chara agreed. Then she cupped her abdomen with her hands and smiled. The first green fingers of spring were beginning to shoot their way up through the thawing ground. Geese flew over hinting at an early spring. All around life was blooming—and soon, another life would spring forth. Chara's face took on a glow that soon had the village women talking.

Chara was a favorite among the village people. She was so shy and sweet, she attracted people like bees to honey. Everywhere she went, she tried to help the people who most needed it. Sometimes she gave food, sometimes she helped with housework, sometimes she cared for children while a tired mother had some time to rest. Because of her help, many were willing to listen when she talked to them of her God, which she did tirelessly.

Decimus smiled as he watched his wife. His sister too had succumbed to her charm. As Chara's pregnancy progressed, so did Eudemia's mothering.

He had to admit, though, his own heart was filled with dread for the pain he knew Chara would have to bear. He continually prayed that God would keep her safe.

❧

The trees were in full bloom and summer was full upon them when Galla rode into the village. Heads turned as he walked his horse through the village and headed it up the hill without stopping.

Eudemia saw him coming before anyone else. Throwing down the rag she was using to wipe the table, she ran outside and met him as his horse came to a stop.

"Galla."

He slid from his horse. He stood there a long time, his hands curling and uncurling at his side.

Decimus came running from the fields behind the house where he was tending the crops. Throwing his arms around Galla, he hugged him hard. "We've missed you, you old horse. Come on in, come on in."

Galla followed him inside, intensely aware of Eudemia only three steps behind him.

"Chara!" Decimus bellowed. "Come see!"

Chara hurried from the back of the house, her brows lifting in surprise. Her eyes sparkled with delight as she threw her arms around Galla's neck.

He smiled wryly, noticing her gently rounded stomach. "You seem to have grown a bit since I last saw you."

Blushing, she threw him a pretend pout. "What a thing to say to a woman. Are you becoming a barbarian, Galla?"

He grinned fully. "I always have been."

The news Galla brought them was not good. "I foresee much bloodshed," he told them, his face grim.

"And what of you, did you accomplish what you set out to do?"

Although Chara asked the question, Galla was watching Eudemia. "I resigned my commission in the army. I know General Galba, so I'm confident my resignation will be accepted."

"Did you find your people?"

He nodded at Decimus. "Cadwaladyr caught up with me and led me home."

Eudemia frowned. "Where is Cadwaladyr?"

Galla sighed heavily. "He decided to stay with the Trinovantes for the time being. They are arming themselves for battle and it seems they will be the first to attack."

Eudemia's soft voice penetrated the silence that followed his words. "And then we will follow."

Shrugging, Galla got to his feet. "Maybe. Maybe not. Let's not borrow trouble. God has worked miracles before. No matter what happens, my trust is in the Lord."

Decimus rose to his feet also. "We have some good news for you, my friend."

Galla looked at Chara. "So I see."

Chara blushed. "Not *that* good news." Turning, she took Eudemia's hand. "Eudemia has accepted Christ as her Savior. She and Cadvan both."

Since Eudemia was looking down, she didn't see the joy that filled Galla's eyes. "I'm pleased," he said softly. The tone of his voice brought Eudemia's eyes flying to his.

Exchanging glances, Decimus and Chara excused themselves. Galla watched them walk away. When he turned back to Eudemia, she had already turned from him.

Taking her by the arms, he turned her back to face him. She looked in his eyes and her breath caught in her throat. Such love shone from their dark brown depths that tears sprang to her eyes.

"I need to explain," he told her softly.

She shook her head. "No. Chara explained it to me. You could not marry an unbeliever."

He nodded. "That is so, but as a centurion in Rome's army, I was forbidden to marry, also."

She looked in his eyes, her own full of questions.

"If you still love me, Eudemia, I would like you to marry me."

A slow smile spread across her face. Her eyes began to glow and Galla pulled her close. Burying his face in her hair, he thanked God for all He had done. What the Apostle Paul had said was true. Everything had worked together for their good.

Cadvan burst through the door, halting on the threshold. His eyes rapidly searched the room, landing at last on Galla. With a cry, he threw himself into Galla's arms.

Eudemia smiled, tears misting her eyes. Looking up, she caught Galla's tender look. A knot formed in her throat. Nodding her head, she smiled.

"We'll be glad to marry you, Galla."

epilogue

The Romans first invaded Britannia in 55 B.C. and they conquered Gaul the same year. The Celts lived on both sides of the English channel, and druidism was practiced in Gaul as well as Britannia. The Romans especially hated the druids and tried to eliminate them; the druids, however, continued to keep a hold on the people for almost two hundred years.

Although the Romans tried to annihilate the druids and their religion, no amount of force could accomplish this. What the Roman army with all their might was not able to achieve, a carpenter from Galilee did.

As Christianity spread slowly through the region, many of the polytheistic religions died. Christians fleeing the persecution of Rome headed for Britannia where Rome's army was not as powerful. As they flowed over the countryside, God's love went with them.

This story transpires from A.D. 67 through A.D. 68. After Nero died, Rome had a difficult time. Over the next thirty years they had six caesars which caused much chaos in the empire. Troops were recalled from the outer regions of the empire to reinforce and protect Rome's emperor.

Although Rome eventually conquered all of Britannia, only God could conquer the druids.

A Letter To Our Readers

Dear Reader:

In order that we might better contribute to your reading enjoyment, we would appreciate your taking a few minutes to respond to the following questions. When completed, please return to the following:

Rebecca Germany, Managing Editor
Heartsong Presents
P.O. Box 719
Uhrichsville, Ohio 44683

1. Did you enjoy reading *Edge of Destiny?*
   ❑ Very much. I would like to see more books
     by this author!
   ❑ Moderately
     I would have enjoyed it more if _____

   _____

2. Are you a member of **Heartsong Presents**? ❑Yes ❑No
   If no, where did you purchase this book?_____

   _____

3. What influenced your decision to purchase this
   book? (Check those that apply.)

   ❑ Cover   ❑ Back cover copy

   ❑ Title   ❑ Friends

   ❑ Publicity   ❑ Other_____

4. How would you rate, on a scale from 1 (poor) to 5
   (superior), the cover design?_____

5. On a scale from 1 (poor) to 10 (superior), please rate the following elements.

    ___Heroine   ___Plot

    ___Hero   ___Inspirational theme

    ___Setting   ___Secondary characters

6. What settings would you like to see covered in **Heartsong Presents** books?_____

_____

_____

7. What are some inspirational themes you would like to see treated in future books?_____

_____

_____

8. Would you be interested in reading other **Heartsong Presents** titles?   ❑ Yes   ❑ No

9. Please check your age range:
   ❑ Under 18   ❑ 18-24   ❑ 25-34
   ❑ 35-45   ❑ 46-55   ❑ Over 55

10. How many hours per week do you read? _____

Name _____

Occupation _____

Address _____

City_____ State_____ Zip _____

WHEN I'M ON MY KNEES

Anita Corrine Donihue

Prayers especially for women, prayers that emanate from the heart, prayers that deal with friendship, family, and peace. Packaged in a beautifully printed leatherette cover, women will also find hymns and poems that focus on prayer in their everyday lives.

About the author:
Anita Corrine Donihue, a teacher with thirty years of experience, is the coauthor of *Apples for a Teacher* and *Joy to the World,* two very popular titles from Barbour Books.

(212 pages, Leatherette, 4" x 6¾")

······ Heart♥ng ······

HISTORICAL ROMANCE IS CHEAPER BY THE DOZEN!

Any 12 *Heartsong Presents* titles for only $26.95 *

*plus $1.00 shipping and handling per order and sales tax where applicable.

Buy any assortment of twelve *Heartsong Presents* titles and save 25% off of the already discounted price of $2.95 each!

HEARTSONG PRESENTS TITLES AVAILABLE NOW:

(If ordering from this page, please remember to include it with the order form.)

······················

Hearts♥ng Presents
Love Stories Are Rated G!

That's for godly, gratifying, and of course, great! If you love a thrilling love story, but don't appreciate the sordidness of some popular paperback romances, **Heartsong Presents** is for you. In fact, **Heartsong Presents** is the *only inspirational romance book club*, the only one featuring love stories where Christian faith is the primary ingredient in a marriage relationship.

Sign up today to receive your first set of four, never before published Christian romances. Send no money now; you will receive a bill with the first shipment. You may cancel at any time without obligation, and if you aren't completely satisfied with any selection, you may return the books for an immediate refund!

Imagine. . .four new romances every four weeks—two historical, two contemporary—with men and women like you who long to meet the one God has chosen as the love of their lives. . .all for the low price of $9.97 postpaid.

To join, simply complete the coupon below and mail to the address provided. **Heartsong Presents** romances are rated G for another reason: They'll arrive *Godspeed!*